MW01502985

The
TORCH
of TRUTH

The
TORCH
of TRUTH

by Edith S. Witmer

Cover design by Matt Feener

Rod and Staff Publishers, Inc.
P.O. Box 3, Hwy. 172
Crockett, Kentucky 41413
Telephone: 606-522-4348

ISBN 978-07399-2441-9

Catalog no. 2436

1   2   3   4   5   —   21   20   19   18   17   16   15   14   13   12

To the children God has given us
—Sarah, Ray, and Daryl—
with the fervent prayer that they also
will pass the "torch of truth"
to their children.

Preface

Jesus said, "I am the vine, ye are the branches: He that abideth in me, and I in him, the same bringeth forth much fruit: for without me ye can do nothing" (John 15:5). Christ calls us to a life filled with His Spirit and set apart from the world to follow Him in holiness. When we abide in Christ, we have fellowship with Him and our lives become living sacrifices that spread God's message to a fallen world.

John wrote the following message from the Lord to the church at Sardis: "Be watchful, and strengthen the things which remain, that are ready to die: for I have not found thy works perfect before God. Remember therefore how thou hast received and heard, and hold fast, and repent. If therefore thou shalt not watch, I will come on thee as a thief, and thou shalt not know what hour I will come upon thee. Thou hast a few names even in Sardis which have not defiled their garments; and they shall walk with me in white: for they are worthy" (Revelation 3:2–4).

John and Edna Troyer and their friends find themselves in a church setting similar to Sardis, where many things are ready to die, or had already done so. Like many of us in the past, they find themselves desiring spiritual fellowship for encouragement and growth in their Christian lives.

Although some members of the church are still faithful, godly people, the Troyers realize that the main influence of their congregation will take them and their family down a road they do not want to travel.

Most readers will equate the various church settings in the story with the churches in their experience. However, this story is not intended to downgrade or venerate any particular church group. The conditions depicted, both positive and negative, exist in many church groups. Any faithful church needs to recognize that false teaching and sinful practices will arise in their midst. "Also of your own selves shall men arise, speaking perverse things, to draw away disciples after them" (Acts 20:30).

The Scriptures have a remedy for this. The church is responsible to faithfully identify unsound teaching—teaching that fails to bring forth the fruits of righteousness—and to stop the leavening influence of the erring. "Now I beseech you, brethren, mark them which cause divisions and offences contrary to the doctrine which ye have learned; and avoid them (Romans 16:17). "Know ye not that a little leaven leaveneth the whole lump?" (1 Corinthians 5:6). "Whose mouths must be stopped, who subvert whole houses, teaching things which they ought not"(Titus 1:11).

Although it is the responsibility of every faithful church to help a sinner find repentance or to purge out the leaven of unsound doctrine, some churches claim the authority to discipline yet fail to deal with carnality and a lack of holiness in their members. These churches are the most likely to abuse the Biblical teachings on avoidance.

The church must carry a strong message of holiness in daily life and an appreciation for conservative values as well as being spiritually alive to God. God does not give us the option of choosing one and leaving the others. In this story, you will observe how wrong choices pave the road to apostasy, and how right choices lead to God's blessing.

May we be faithful to the Lord who has called us!

—*David Mast*

Introduction

What does God want from His children? What does He require from His church? How may we please Him? Most importantly, how can we know the heart of God?

This book is born out of a deep grief for the chasms that people coming from conservative churches fall into as they search for answers to these questions. The world yields many soft, seductive frameworks that tend to affect the way we think and reason. Therefore, a stalwart stand on the truth of God's Word is the only way to be prepared for His coming. We must know who God is, what He hates, and what He loves.

Jesus said, "Ye are my friends, if ye do whatsoever I command you" (John 15:14). As born-again children of God, it is our privilege to live consecrated lives of holiness, for to be godly is to be like God! Christ has already secured the promise that He will bless His own with more than the world can ever offer. Eternal life, with all its freedom, springs from the heart of God Himself.

Christ longs for fellowship with His own. During His mission on earth, Jesus entreated His Father, "That they all may be one; as thou, Father, art in me, and I in thee, that they also may be one in us" (John 17:21). God created man for fellowship, and it is His ultimate goal to share a blissful eternity with us in heaven.

As the bride of Christ, we bow humbly to worship our Lord, who said, "I am the vine, ye are the branches: He that abideth in me, and I in him, the same bringeth forth much fruit: for without me ye can do nothing" (John 15:5).

God requires that both our hearts and our lives be aligned with Him. We cannot choose between form and content, for the signature of God in our hearts will produce a life that is starkly different from a permissive world. When we are a part of Christ's vine, His love will flow from our hearts in vibrant fruitfulness.

As we take God seriously, we will want to identify with a Scriptural, disciplined body of believers who worship God as living sacrifices. Then our churches and our lives will step out to stand radically with God. May we follow on to know Him!

—*Eldon and Edith Witmer*

The
TORCH
of TRUTH

"I am the vine,
ye are the branches:
He that abideth in me,
and I in him,
the same bringeth forth much fruit:
for without me ye can do nothing."
John 15:5

CHAPTER 1

John Troyer whistled cheerfully as he turned onto Shoemaker Road. The morning was fresh, and he smiled as he gave his spirited mare slack reins. Shoulders erect, he scanned the countryside, dotted with cornfields, barns, and fenced pastures.

His thoughts ran ahead to the Bible study planned for that evening. He and Edna enjoyed those Bible studies so much! If they managed everything well, there would be just enough time to eat supper, get the three children ready, and hop into the surrey for the twenty-minute ride to Abner Miller's home. His mare, Lady, would cover the miles quickly.

So much had happened in the last three years—and so much before that! Unconsciously, a frown puckered John's forehead as he remembered the wild oats he had sown in his teenage years. How he had grieved his godly father—and his Father in heaven! But in a meandering path, he had finally found God, like the prodigal son, and had made peace with both his heavenly Father and his earthly father. He and Edna had found peace three years ago, on the day they buried little Matthew. His thought train ended abruptly as he turned into Miller's Cabinet Shop. He unhitched Lady, tied her in the barn, and headed into the office to clock in.

"Good morning, John!"

John turned to face Abner Miller, and a smile broke over his face. "Are you still looking for us and James tonight?"

"We sure are!" returned Abner. "Emma said to tell you all to come in time for supper. Then we can have the Bible study afterward."

"Good enough," answered John.

The whir of saws and the hum of sandpaper filled John's ears as he entered the shop. Taking his work orders from Abner, he began cutting out pieces to assemble frames.

"Daddy's home!" shouted four-year-old Rachel. Paul dropped his toy truck and hurried to the door.

"Hi, everybody." John smiled as he came in the door. He scooped up the baby, while Rachel and Paul each grabbed a pant leg. Edna stood at the stove, watching the tussle and laughing.

"Welcome home. How was your day?" she asked above the hubbub.

"One of the saw motors burned out today," John returned. "But other than that, good. Was Hannah still fussy today?" He lifted the baby's face. "Here, let me see," he said. "Did your new tooth come through yet?"

"Not quite," Edna replied. "But we made out. I just

didn't get much work done."

"Mama read us lots of stories while she held Hannah," Rachel explained.

John met Edna's eyes tenderly. His heart filled with gratitude. That was just the way Edna was—sweet, calm, and steady under stress.

A warm glow filled Edna's eyes. "And now we're glad you're home," she said. "We've been waiting for that all day."

"Abner said Emma is expecting us for supper," John continued. "I said we would come. Is that all right with you?"

"Sure. That is just like Emma to invite us all," Edna said. "I'll use this food for supper tomorrow night."

In twenty minutes they were all settled in the surrey. John signaled Lady to start, and she trotted out the lane.

Edna looked up into John's face. "Do you ever think how much you will miss this horse if we start driving a car?"

John nodded pensively. "Yes," he said, "sometimes I do. She took us places during our courtship and has been pulling us for five years since our marriage." John glanced back at Rachel and Paul in the back seat and little Hannah sitting on her mother's lap. "These children have never known us to have another horse. Well, I don't know," he continued. "But sometimes I think that time could be soon. Maybe my father will want Lady."

"So many things to think about . . ." mused Edna.

"Yes," said John, "and we won't do anything until we are sure of God's leading. So far the church here at Shady Glen has allowed us to have our Bible studies, and that helps to feed us spiritually."

Edna nodded. "Yes. I don't know what I would do

without those. It's not only the truths we find in the Bible but also the fellowship and the sharing with Abner's and James."

"Can you imagine that it has been only three years since we have come to really know God?"

Edna breathed deeply of the fragrant evening air. "Yes and no," she returned. "But it all started before that. You know how we started thinking seriously after the twins were born. Then during the long year of Matthew's sickness, I watched him suffer and had hours to think while I rocked him." She paused and then said soberly, "It hurts more to see your child suffer than to suffer yourself."

John nodded mutely.

"Each day that I cared for Matthew, though he didn't know that I was caring for him, I came to realize how much more God loved me than I loved Matthew. And I wasn't responding to that."

John reflected quietly. When he spoke, his voice was husky. "God was working deeply in my heart during the year of Matthew's sickness too," he said. "But it wasn't until after the funeral that we repented and finally committed ourselves completely to God. And our lives have been different ever since."

For a few moments the only sound was the clip clop of Lady's hooves. Then a sigh escaped John's lips. "And since we've come to God, I continue to ponder the church life God wants us to have. We've been realizing we may not always be able to stay at Shady Glen. If God directs us to leave, are you at peace about making the changes we would probably make to fit in with a spiritual, conservative congregation—something like the conservative Mennonite churches we know about?"

"I think I am, John," answered Edna. "Are you?"

"Yes," answered John. "In the past years I've been pondering heavily how we can be faithful to God, and what church standards God wants us to keep. I believe we could be faithful in another church, and receive the spiritual nurture we are longing for. A committed life will always bow in obedience to the God it loves. Our lives are bound up in Jesus Christ."

"Yes!" John could hear the smile in Edna's voice. " 'The blood of Jesus Christ . . . cleanseth us from all sin.' "

The Bible study was nearly over. As John had led the study on John 14, Edna's heart reached out like a thirsty garden for the tender comfort of God's love.

"Thank You, God, for the gift of Yourself," she prayed quietly.

As Abner Miller closed the meeting, he paused a moment and then cleared his throat. "And now I have something to share that I did not want to say at the beginning," he said slowly. "We know how much these little services have meant to all of us and how we have been learning so much together. Well, on Sunday Bishop Sam came to see me. He was very kind and respectful, but he said that our ministry here at Shady Glen has been talking about our Bible study. They have been receiving complaints from the congregation about our having Bible studies, and the ministry feels we are creating an in-group—a group within a group—which is true. And they are asking us to stop meeting."

A general gasp broke out in the room.

James Miller was the first to speak. He glanced at John, then at Abner. "John and I are both young, Abner. What do you think we should do?"

"Well," said Abner, "up to this point we have not been working against the ministry's direction here at Shady Glen, so I do not feel we have been in the wrong. But now, if we continue to meet for Bible studies, we will be in violation. What do you think? Do we want to work with them and stop having our Bible study? Or is this a signal from God that it is time for us to step out in order to continue our journey with Him?"

"Where would we go for church fellowship?" asked John.

"We may not all do the same thing," Abner continued, "but we will want to keep following God and focusing on Him. We will want to worship with believers who obey God's Word. We could move to another community, or we could consider another congregation here within a reasonable distance."

"How much do we want a church with rules?" asked James.

Abner thought for a time before he spoke. "For my part, I believe the Spirit of God, written in the heart, makes rules unnecessary. At Shady Glen, we have all seen a strong use of rules. People simply choose to do or not to do what the preachers tell them to do. Many of the people do not even know God. Following a simple lifestyle will not save us. Seeking salvation through a simple life leaves empty hearts. You know how the young people dance, drink, and use drugs and then expect to settle down later. I want Christianity that obeys God from the heart."

"I agree that we cannot be saved simply by following a written standard," said John. "But then, how will we keep from losing out when our own ideas and concepts of God could cause us to think we are standing with God—when we really are not? Don't we need a church body with some guidelines to give us stability?"

"God is faithful," answered Abner, "and He is able to keep us faithful."

John's brow puckered as he pondered the thought. When he spoke, his voice was quiet. "I'm not doubting God. The person I doubt is myself. Don't brethren and sisters need each other, to help them find their way?"

"Yes," said James, "I wonder about that too. We need practical applications that are based on the Bible. As Christians, the forms that we practice and the contents of our hearts must come together in harmony. If we're going to be separated to God and hate sin, we'll want to lead godly lives, with a godly way of doing things.

"Here at Shady Glen, we have seen a strong emphasis on form without the contents of the heart being given to God. Now I challenge myself not to fall into the opposite trap—that of dropping form—as I focus on the contents of the heart."

"I wonder," John said thoughtfully, "if it is right for a man to believe that he has the ultimate authority to lead his family, without a strong sense of accountability to a brotherhood? Is one man that dependable?"

Abner's voice was calm as he replied, "I understand all the thoughts you are sharing. We have been going through those too. And I will respect the decisions each of you makes. I think each family should decide for themselves, rather than our making a joint decision."

John and James nodded their assent.

"Then we all feel it is best to stop our studies for the time being?" Abner asked.

"I believe that would be the right thing to do," John answered. "If we cannot have our needs met here, then it is probably time to move on."

"You feel the same way, James?" Abner asked.

"I do," James returned.

"Very well," said Abner. "Before we part, let's spend time in prayer, asking God for direction. I know He will give it to us."

Edna's tears fell onto Hannah's dress as she prayed. Everyone wept. This Bible study group had been an oasis of encouragement for them all. And now the future held such hard questions and uncertainties.

"We'll keep in touch, Edna," Emma said softly as they parted. "Abner and I will be praying for you and John."

Edna squeezed her hand. Emma's motherly heart was comforting. "That means so much," she replied. "We will do the same for you."

"What will we do, John?" Edna asked after the children were in bed that night.

"Well," said John, "we will continue to seek God. And

we will use our best God-given judgment, not the impulse of our emotions. I think I see what Father means when he tells us not to throw away our spiritual birthright if we leave the church here at Shady Glen. So many people leave a heavily regimented church, thinking that no rules mean spiritual freedom. Then they think that spiritual freedom means doing what they want to . . . and they walk into the world. But true freedom comes from doing God's will and being free from sin."

"We already want to do God's will," said Edna. "So why should we mind church regulations that help us to understand what God's will is?"

"I feel the same way," John agreed. "If we don't move, we have about three choices of congregations to attend. The Living Waters congregation has no rules, and we would be free to do whatever we feel God is telling us to do. Meadow Brook has some rules, but still seems to be alive and open. And then there's Pine Ridge, where everyone does things pretty much the same way. I'm not sure if I like that. They do seem spiritual, but it scares me a little."

Edna sighed. "Whatever we do, let's not drift into the world. This decision will affect these little children tremendously in the coming years."

John lay awake for an hour, searching for answers. "God," he prayed, "help me to lead my family faithfully!"

CHAPTER 2

Edna's slight form leaned forward over the stove as she flipped pancakes.

"Mm-m!" exclaimed John as he came in the back door. "In a few months we'll be butchering our pig. Then we'll have sausage or bacon to go with those pancakes!"

"I will be glad for meat to can again," Edna answered. Butchering time was a busy but pleasant time of working together. "I wonder who will help us butcher this year, John."

"You mean if we are under the ban?"

Edna nodded.

"Well, I don't know. But I don't think all of our family will forsake us. Do you want to tell your parents what we're doing?"

"Yes," Edna answered. "They have been good parents to me, and I think it would be respectful to be open with them. I don't know if my father is a Christian. But Mother is. She made sure we all knew how to become Christians, and she is concerned about spiritual things—even though she doesn't talk about them very much. But what do you think they will say?"

"I don't know," answered John. "But we will be open with them, and we won't argue or try to prove anything. Our lives will need to tell the story. We'll just share what we believe the Lord wants us to do and ask for their advice. And then we'll listen to anything they have to say. Shall we go tonight?"

Hannah's cry came from the bedroom. Edna turned to get the baby. "That suits me fine, John," she answered.

Edna pulled nervously on the fringed end of the lap robe as the surrey pulled onto the highway.

"Where shall we go first, John," she queried, "your home or mine?"

"You choose."

"Your home then," Edna returned.

"All right. They already know what we're thinking anyway. So that seems a little easier.

"You know, Edna. Both of our families really do care about us. In some way or other, our decision will bring pain into our families. Let's make sure we are humble and approachable so we can do our part to have good relationships."

"Do you think we can still have good relationships?" asked Edna.

"I don't know," answered John. "Probably with mine. Maybe not with yours."

Edna looked at the well-kept flower beds as she walked onto the porch of her in-law's house. She had always been welcome here, yet tonight her heart caught in her throat. John knocked. The door opened, and John, Sr., stood in the doorway.

Seeing the gravity on John's face, he surveyed the family for an instant. Then he said calmly, "Come on in, son."

Edna walked in the door. "Good evening, Mother!" she ventured.

Grace Troyer's gentle face warmed as she lifted Hannah. "We're so glad you came," she said, smiling at Edna. "Father and I were just praying for you."

John gazed tenderly at the faces of his parents. How long they had prayed for him, through his years of sin while he dabbled in rock music, drugs, and alcohol. Father had always taught the family from the Bible. They had always been there for him, the youngest of twelve children. Somehow, there was no need for preliminaries.

"Father and Mother," John began, after the children settled down to play at the other end of the room, "Edna and I have something we want to share with you and to ask your advice about."

"Yes?" queried John, Sr.

"You know how Edna and I found the Lord after Matthew died and how we are trying to follow Him now. We feel that the time has come for us to leave Shady Glen. Do you have any advice to give us?"

John, Sr., looked grave. He stroked his beard and gazed at his wife for a long moment. She nodded, and he turned to face John and Edna.

"We knew this was coming, though in a way it startles us." John, Sr., spoke quietly, measuring his words. Then he continued, "We understand what you have been going through since you came to know the Lord, and that you are having a problem finding fulfillment in the church here. So we will not stand in your way. But we do have some advice for you."

"What is it, Father?" John asked as he leaned forward attentively.

"Go without bitterness or resentment. Do not argue with people or defend yourselves. Let your lives be your testimony.

"You are leaving a church with strict requirements," he continued. "But the lack of spirituality here does not mean that rules are wrong. In the last ten years, I have seen a dozen families leave and lose themselves or their children to the world. It is necessary to be both spiritual and holy, and rules are good when they help us to lead holy lives. So don't lose your spiritual birthright, as I told you before. Remain committed to Christ Jesus. Keep Biblical applications, and appreciate conservative values. They will help you to remain stable."

"We want to remember that, Father," John said, almost reverently. "Are you planning to leave too?"

"No, not as we're thinking now," answered John, Sr. "Mother and I are almost too old to do something like that. There are people we can touch here, and we plan to stay. We will pray for each other."

"Will you shun us?" Edna asked hesitantly.

John, Sr., shook his head, and Edna breathed more easily.

"Will you pray for us now, Father?" John asked quietly.

His father nodded.

John turned around to kneel. Suddenly it struck him. This rocker was the one his mother had used to rock him to sleep. He bowed his head, and tears flowed unashamedly down his cheeks.

"Our Father in heaven," prayed John, Sr., "we ask You to be with John, Edna, and their little ones. You know the situation they find themselves in and the choices they are making. Give them wisdom and understanding, and give them hearts that will always obey You. If they err, cause them to know and turn back to the right. Lord, we ask You to help them find the fellowship that they need, and use them for Your honor and glory. Give them the Spirit of Christ, and lead them surely as they decide what to do from here. In Jesus' Name. Amen."

The presence of God had come to meet them. For a full minute, no one moved. Edna remained with bowed head as her heart burned.

Quietly, John and Edna picked up the children and prepared to leave.

"Be faithful, and remember that we will be praying for you," Grace said quietly as they parted.

The surrey wheels hummed quietly as the family headed toward the next stop. Edna gazed at the stars. Then she turned to John.

"I almost wish we wouldn't get there," she whispered. "I want you to talk, John."

"All right," agreed John. "We'll ask Father and Mother to come outside to talk. The children can stay inside with Elizabeth.

"We will try to be honorable," he continued. "We are doing the right thing to talk to your parents. We will be as kind and respectful to them as we can be. They are concerned about us."

"I know they are," agreed Edna. "I hate to hurt them. I wonder if any of the other married children will be home."

Mary greeted them at the door. "What a nice surprise!" she said. "Come in."

Edna smiled at her mother. She drank in the comfort of the kitchen, with its warm, lived-in look. Yet it was tidy, as her mother always left it. She greeted Henry, Elizabeth, and Steven. How they were all growing! Henry was almost twenty, and Elizabeth and Steven would soon be sixteen.

Edna turned to receive her father's strong handshake. She swallowed as she looked into his warm brown eyes. How long would she be welcome here?

"Father," John ventured after the children were busy with the toy box, "would you and Mother please come outside with us? We have something to share with you."

A ring of tension circled the room, and Sam Yoder started slightly. Then he checked himself. "All right," he said. "Are you ready, Mother?"

"Yes, John?" Sam queried as they stood under the stars.

"We wanted to share something with you and ask your advice," John began a bit hesitantly. He paused and cleared his throat. Then he began again. "You know how Edna and I found the Lord about a year ago. We have been following the Lord and are really enjoying learning more about God's will for our lives."

"Did Bishop Sam ask you to stop having your Bible studies?" Sam asked.

"Yes," answered John. "We feel the time has come for us to leave the church here at Shady Glen. We plan to stay Biblical and conservative. We wanted you to know what we are planning, and we would like to hear any advice you have to give us."

Mary gasped as the impact of John's words struck her. How she loved Edna! The road ahead would be hard because they would be expected to shun her. Covering her face with her hands, she sobbed heartbrokenly.

In the moonlight, John thought he saw his father-in-law's face turn gray, and for a brief moment, he swayed. When Sam spoke, his voice was husky.

"Well," he said, "thank you for telling us. We do care about you. But I wouldn't do it. Most people who leave lose everything. Think about your children." He paused. "And you know we will have to shun you," he finished hoarsely. "That will be so hard!"

A silence that was heavier than words almost strangled Edna.

"I'm so sorry to hurt you, Mother and Father," she said between sobs. "You have been good parents to me, and I will always love you."

As she thought about it later, Edna hardly knew how they left. But she remembered her mother's parting words. "Come over to spend the day before you are in the ban."

"Edna," said John as they sipped tea at home, "are you still willing to move ahead with our decision?"

"Yes, John. What else can we do? Have you changed your mind?"

"No," he answered. "I was just checking to make sure we're still together. Then the next thing will be to visit Bishop Sam."

Edna nodded mutely.

Late that night, long after Edna was asleep, John remained on his knees beside the bed, beseeching God for wisdom and guidance. At last he joined Edna and fell into a peaceful sleep.

Chapter 3

John looked at the clock on the wall as the hum of the drum sander filled his ears. He finger-tested the boards he had sanded for smoothness. It would take only one more pass.

He looked up as the five-minute warning bell roared into his ears. Another workweek was over. One by one, the machines were turned off. Laughter and lively conversation filled the shop as the men tidied the workplace.

"You're still going over to Bishop Sam's place on the way home?" Abner asked as John checked out in the office.

"Yes," said John.

"I'll be praying for you," Abner assured him. "I went over last night."

"How did it go?"

"Emma and I went over together," Abner answered. "I guess it went about the way I expected. Bishop Sam was respectful. Though we won't be getting a church letter, I believe it is still more honorable for us to withdraw our membership than to violate the church discipline."

"What are you thinking about church membership now, Abner?" John asked.

Abner paused and frowned in concentration. "I'm looking for church life that focuses on the inner experience," he said. "I don't think we need the trappings of tradition to do that. If the heart is right, then everything that flows from the heart will be right.

"I'm not against plain suits, John, but have you ever found a verse in the Bible that says a man should wear one? Or that you have to make a dress in one particular way? Does using a radio with caution need to be wrong? We place so many burdens on people when we have preconceived ideas." He stopped abruptly and looked at John. "What are you thinking by now?" he asked.

John spoke quietly. " 'Follow holiness, without which no man shall see the Lord,' " he quoted. "I understand your thought that our Christianity must come from the heart. But what about being set apart for God in our lives? Does not a Biblical standard of discipline help us to do that? I'm not wearing a plain suit because it saves me, but because I want to be identified with godly people—who wear that instead of a worldly suit or casual clothes.

"It's true that the Bible doesn't have the word *radio* or *Internet* in it, and it doesn't say exactly how we should dress. But the principles for holiness in all those areas are found in the Bible. A Scriptural, written discipline helps us put those principles to work in our lives and safeguards us from the snares around us. I look upon conservative values as a blessing."

"Well," said Abner, "we remain brethren. May God give us each wisdom to guide our families."

John walked into the barn nearby and hitched up to go home. He was glad that the workday was over. He and Edna were fasting today. His body was weary, but his heart was at peace.

Bishop Sam looked up and propped the pitchfork he was using against the wall as John walked into his horse barn.

"Well," he said, smiling, "it's good to see you, John. Sit down," he added, pointing to a bale of hay. "What brings you here?"

John sat down on the bale of hay opposite the bishop and looked at Bishop Sam. He respected the aged man. For years he had seen Bishop Sam stand in front of the church, leading the congregation. When John and Edna had come to God and cleared past sin with the church, he had rejoiced with them. And now John was here to terminate Bishop Sam's responsibility for himself. John looked into the kind gray eyes surveying him.

"Bishop Sam," John began, "you know how Edna and I found the Lord."

The bishop nodded. "Yes," he said. "Go on."

"Well," said John, "we want to go on serving God, and we're finding that we can't really fit into the church here at Shady Glen anymore. Our souls want spiritual light and fellowship that we haven't found here."

"I'm sorry to hear that, John." Bishop Sam dropped his head and sighed heavily. "It's genuine people like you that we need."

Silence hung between them, and for a full minute no one spoke.

"What I came to say is that Edna and I are planning to seek membership in another church," John said, a catch in his throat. "What is our next step in doing that?"

"We can't give you a church letter," Bishop Sam answered. "But what you're doing now informs us of your intentions."

John nodded mutely.

"You are aware that this will mean that you will be under the ban?" Bishop Sam asked quietly. "That you will not be able to sit at the same table with our people or receive things from their hands?"

"We understand that," said John. "It will be hard, but we believe this is what God wants us to do."

Bishop Sam spoke heavily. "This will not be announced at church until two weeks from this coming Sunday. So if you change your mind, let me know before then."

John waved as he backed Lady from where she was tied beside the barn and headed out the lane. As he turned onto the road, he looked back. Bishop Sam was still watching him, his shoulders stooped.

Edna met John at the door. She waited quietly until he walked to the closet and hung up his hat. When he still did not speak, she raised the question.

"Did you talk to Bishop Sam?"

"Yes," said John. "He was very sad. He said they need people like us. He said the ban won't be announced until two weeks from this Sunday."

"My mother sent me a letter today," shared Edna. "Remember how she told me to come spend a day with her before we are put under the ban? She wants me to come over to make doughnuts on Monday."

"Good," John answered a bit absently. "Maybe you should invite her to do something with you the next week. She dearly loves these little children. After two weeks they probably won't spend a lot of time with us."

"Oh, John!" Edna exclaimed as the magnitude of John's visit to Bishop Sam struck her.

Edna fed the children supper while John took care of the chores. After she put the baby to bed and busied Rachel and Paul with toys, she slipped off to the bedroom to join her husband as he knelt in prayer beside the bed.

"Dear God," prayed John, "please be with us. We need Your direction and Your blessing. Guide our hearts and minds, and help us to be completely humble and open before You. Help us to know You, for You are truth. Give us Your torch of truth! Teach us to follow Your will.

"You know the pain our hearts feel and the joy we also sense as we follow You. We are like Peter as he stepped out of the boat to walk on the water. Be with our families in their pain, and help us to bless them."

After Edna prayed aloud, she and John still knelt quietly, pouring out their hearts before God.

Edna smiled as she placed the bowl of steaming potato soup on the table for lunch. Saturdays were special days for the whole family, since John was home that day.

"Are you hungry, Paul?" John asked as he lifted the little boy onto his booster seat.

"Yeth! Me hungry!" Paul nodded vigorously.

The family bowed their heads for prayer.

"Edna," said John, "I have about two hours to help pick the beans this afternoon. What time is best?"

"Wonderful!" exclaimed Edna, her eyes shining. "After the children are in bed for naps would be good."

"Suits me fine," answered John. "I'll clean out Lady's pen until then."

John and Edna had just finished picking the second row of beans when a buggy crunched in the driveway.

"It's Stephen and Thelma!" John exclaimed. "It's good to see them again." He carried the buckets of beans under the oak tree and hurried over to the buggy.

"Welcome!" he called. "We're just ready to start snapping these beans. Can you stay a while?"

"Hello," answered Stephen. "We can stay a little. We just stopped in on our way back from town."

Edna smiled into Thelma's warm brown eyes. So many memories floated to the surface of her mind. She and John and Stephen and Thelma had all gone to school together, had been in the same youth group, and had joined church about the same time. When they married, they had been wedding attendants for each other.

Edna reached for one of the twins as Stephen and Thelma unloaded their little brood of four children. The beans flew as the couples chatted. After a while there was a lull in the conversation.

"John," said Stephen, "it's coming to us by way of

the grapevine that you are about to leave our church. Is that right?"

John looked into the serious, troubled expression on Stephen's face.

"I guess secrets like that don't stay quiet for long," said John. "Yes, I told Bishop Sam that we are withdrawing our membership. You and Thelma have been our friends for a long time. We're glad to share with you.

"You know how Edna and I found the Lord and how we have been searching for depth in our spiritual journey. We're longing for a spiritually alive church for fellowship."

"You can't find that in our church?" Stephen asked quietly.

"Can you?"

"Well, I'm not sure," said Stephen. "But we're trying. The thing that frightens us is that so many people who leave highly regimented churches don't know how to keep Scriptural values when they leave. They say they are tired of legalism. But spiritual freedom isn't a license to sin. A lot of people just drift into the world and finally lose their way completely."

"You're right, Stephen," John affirmed. "We're concerned about that too. How can we be sure we remain separated unto God as we leave the church here?"

"Stick with a church that deals with sin, John," Stephen answered. "So many churches brush over sin and carnality in the name of understanding and open-mindedness. Go by what the Bible says, instead of your emotions."

"We're really going to miss you," Thelma said sadly. "We won't be able to do much together after you leave."

"We want you to know that as far as we are concerned, you will always be welcome in our home," John answered.

"We know that," Stephen said with deep feeling. "I will remember you as having been a true friend—one of my best friends. You were the one who led me to the Lord, and I will always be grateful to you for that!"

There were tears in Thelma's eyes as they left. John and Edna watched until the buggy drove out of sight.

Edna turned to John with troubled eyes. "It feels so strange, John," she said, "almost as if they came to our funeral or something."

"Well," said John as he stared absently ahead, "maybe to them, they did."

With a sigh, Edna turned back to the beans.

CHAPTER 4

Monday arrived. Edna bustled about the house as she readied the family to go to Grandma Yoder's house for the day. John would drop them all off on his way to work.

"I'm going to play with Elizabeth!" Rachel exclaimed. "I like Elizabeth a lot."

John smiled. "Elizabeth likes you too. I hope you have a happy day."

"I will play with the puppy," Paul added cheerfully.

Edna smiled. "Steven will probably give you a ride on the swing too."

"I like thwing ride!" Paul exclaimed, jumping up and down.

"John," Edna whispered as he helped her down from the surrey at her parents' home, "I'm a little afraid. It almost hurts too much to go in."

"Go and be a blessing," said John, smiling. "You always are."

Edna flashed a grateful smile to her husband. "Yes," she returned. "It doesn't matter what we receive. It's what we give. I'll remember that and try to make this a really special day for Mother."

Mary hurried to the door as Edna approached. "You've come!" she exclaimed. "I have been looking forward to this day." There was a catch in her voice, and she blew her nose. "Come in. Shall Grandma take your coat off, Paul?"

"Yeth!" Paul exclaimed. "Where Theven?"

"Steven is out at the barn," Elizabeth explained. "He'll come in to see you later. Shall Aunt Elizabeth read you a book?"

Edna set Hannah on the floor with some toys and moved to the sink to finish washing the breakfast dishes.

"I have the doughnut dough rising," Mary informed her. "What kind of fillings would you like to put inside the filled ones?"

"I brought some cherry pie filling," Edna offered, "and I always loved your peanut butter cream filling."

Mary smiled gently. "Then we will make some of those. Father likes them too."

"Edna." It was Elizabeth. "Did I show you the quilt I am putting together now? It's the tumbling block pattern."

"No, you didn't. I did one of those too. Remember how it was almost ruined?"

"Yes," Mary returned. "I do remember. Your greens and pinks were so beautiful after you sewed the blocks together, and Steven was almost ready to help you cut them out again. I caught him with the scissors just in time."

"They say I was only five at the time," a deep voice

volunteered as Steven stepped in the back door, "and I think I brought you a bouquet of dandelions afterward to make peace. Is someone talking about me?"

"Just a little," Edna said with a smile. "Paul has been waiting for you. He wants a swing ride."

"Shall Uncle Steven give you a ride?" Steven asked as he picked up Paul. "Here," he said. "I'll make your head touch the ceiling."

Paul crowed as Steven lifted him higher and higher.

"Now, pleathe thwing!" Paul said as Steven put him on the floor again.

The kitchen was quiet as Edna and her mother worked together. Hannah and Paul were napping, and Rachel was outside with Elizabeth.

Her mother broke the silence. "Is this really what you want to do, Edna? Is John making you leave the church?"

"No, he isn't, Mother," Edna replied. "We have been reading the Bible and learning more about what God has for us. We want to be spiritually alive to God and let Him direct our lives."

"You couldn't do that in our church?" questioned Mary.

"Well, not really," Edna answered. "When we first joined the church as members, we felt that we fitted in. But, Mother, we weren't saved. After we came to know the Lord, our hearts' needs were not being satisfied anymore. We feel that God wants us to be part of a holy church, a church that is alive to spiritual things."

"You won't cut your hair and lose everything? I hate to think of the grandchildren being in a worldly home. . . ."

Mary's voice choked as she looked toward the bedroom where the little ones were sleeping.

"No, Mother," Edna returned. "The Bible teaches us to be separate from the world. It teaches us that women should have long, uncut hair. I don't want to cut my hair or to be worldly. By the grace of God, we mean to teach the children to love and serve Him—and to live godly lives ourselves."

"It's just that I worry about you," Mary said. "What if you lose out with God when you go to another church? What if you go farther than you think you will?

"And I will miss you so much when we won't be able to associate with you very much. Father is afraid about the influence you will have on the younger children," Mary finished sadly.

A dagger smote Edna's heart, and she wept with her mother.

"I know it will be hard, Mother," Edna said finally. "Please remember that I will still love you and that you will be welcome at our house anytime."

"Oh, it just tears me up!" Mary sighed. "I love you too, and I always will. Why must things come to this? That I would need to shun my own daughter!"

"We will give it to God," Edna answered. "I don't think there's anything about shunning that would keep you from praying for us. Why don't we pray for each other every morning?"

A small light came back into Mary's eyes. "Yes!" she exclaimed. "Of course I will do that. I have prayed for you every day since you were born."

"I never knew that," Edna replied. "Thank you for telling me."

"And I always will," said Mary. "I just wanted you to know that when we shun you, it will be more because of Father than me. And remember that Father's heart is in deep pain. I think that's why he has been out in the barn most of the day. He feels that he is losing you. It cuts like a knife, and yet he feels that he has to shun you with the rest of the church. So don't take it personally."

"I'll remember that," Edna said, placing a kiss on her mother's cheek.

Edna missed her father's booming voice throughout the day. In the few personal encounters she had with him, she was stunned by the intense hurt that hollowed his eyes.

Edna smiled as she and John sat down to the supper table with her family. Her eyes scanned the dishes. Ham, mashed potatoes, lima beans, coleslaw, and pumpkin pie— all her favorites. Her mother had remembered!

"Oh, Mother!" Edna exclaimed as they prepared to leave. "The supper was so good! I will always remember it."

Mary's eyes smiled knowingly into her daughter's. "I knew you would like it," she said quietly. "I wanted today to be special. And Elizabeth and I will come over to help you house-clean on Tuesday of next week."

"Was it a good day?" John asked as they started home.

"Yes," said Edna, "it was—in a bittersweet sort of way. Mother and I had a good talk. I think Father is feeling the pain even more than she is."

"Mama," asked Rachel from the back seat, "why did

Grandma cry into my hair when she held me on her lap? She never did that before."

Edna looked helplessly at John. How could little ones understand such hard things?

"I guess she was sad," John supplied. "You love Grandma, don't you? Why don't you make a card for her tomorrow to thank her for the nice day?"

"I will!" exclaimed Rachel. "Grandpa usually plays with us, but today he stood out at the barn and watched us play instead. Why?" she asked.

"Maybe he was sad too," John said gently. "He was probably feeling lonesome for you. Why don't you make him a card too?"

"I'll draw a picture of corn candy on his," said Rachel, "because that's the kind of candy he almost always gives me."

"That's a good idea," said John. "Grandpa will like that."

Chapter 5

John sighed contentedly as he settled onto the couch beside Edna. He had finally walked Hannah to sleep and put her to bed for the night.

He smiled at Edna. "Now it's our turn to talk," he said. "I thought you would like to hear what Abner had to say about their visit to Living Waters on Sunday."

"Yes!" exclaimed Edna. "What did he say?"

"Well, quite a bit, really," answered John. "He was excited. He said it was certainly very different from the services we have at Shady Glen—a lot more alive and emotional. They had a lot of testimonies and confessions. He said he sensed a real sincerity in the way the congregation worshiped.

"The message was about salvation by faith. Abner said the speaker preached that salvation comes only through the blood of Jesus."

"What were the people like?" asked Edna.

"Warm and friendly, Abner said," answered John. "They were invited to one of the homes for lunch, and the men had a spiritual discussion as they visited. But there were some things that bothered Abner. He said the song leader had a wedding ring on."

"Really?" said Edna. "Do they allow that?"

"Well, yes and no," answered John. "The men told Abner that not everyone feels the same way about it. Some of the brethren at Living Waters think the couple shouldn't wear wedding rings. Others say they aren't wearing their rings to be jewelry. They say that it's what is in the heart that counts and that only God can judge them.

"Actually, Abner said the couple aren't really members. But they have been going there for five years and are more or less considered a part of the congregation."

"Anything else?" asked Edna.

"Abner said most of the ladies dressed modestly. Emma told him that they used different patterns. Some of them had cape dresses. One lady dresses like the Amish. Others wear a vest-type cape. Some wore jumpers and blouses. A few had loose-fitting bought dresses. And he said there were all kinds of coverings, from lace doilies to handkerchiefs, to flowing veils and Mennonite or Amish coverings.

"Really?" exclaimed Edna, looking up from the sock she was mending. "How would that work?"

"I don't know," answered John. "My question is whether they will keep the principle if their discipline has so much flexibility.

"He said the men wore a variety of clothes. Some wore casual clothes, and some dressed up. A few just wore clean work clothes. A few men still wore plain suitcoats, but nobody had a worldly suit with a tie. Mostly they just wear other jackets to church, Abner said."

John squinted his eyes, deep in thought, and drummed his fingers on the edge of the end table.

"What else did he say?" asked Edna, after a long pause.

"Abner said they teach that you should sense God through your spirit to know if what you are doing is right. They say that if you have peace about something it must be the right thing to do. At the same time, they say that you must obey the Bible. But they don't have any rules except the decisions that are made at brethren's meetings. They don't represent any denomination—they're just Christians."

"That would be different," Edna offered.

"Some people have radios," John continued, "but no members have TVs. Abner said they don't all believe alike on what constitutes divorce and remarriage, though they believe it is wrong to divorce and remarry."

Edna frowned. "Really?" she asked.

John nodded and continued. "Abner said that several men told him that the group at Living Waters stresses that men should seek God and follow Him, and then the wives should look to their husbands for direction."

Edna nodded as she pondered John's words. Then looking up, she asked, "Did you talk to James since Sunday?"

"Yes," said John. "He stopped in at the shop and talked to me at lunchtime. He went to Pine Ridge on Sunday.

"James said that they received him warmly and that the service had a sincere ring to it. He said the message was on being saved and committed to Christ, and walking in obedience as a result of that. The service didn't sound as emotional as the one at Living Waters. But the people were reverent and attentive and seemed to be dedicated. James said it seems solid, and his soul was fed. He plans to go back again next Sunday."

"Pine Ridge is a fairly conservative Mennonite church, isn't it?"

"Yes," answered John. "It is. I like a church with a safe standard of discipline, because I think that makes a church more stable. We want a church that will be there for our children. But I'm not sure if we want more freedom than they have at Pine Ridge or not."

"Like what?" asked Edna.

Edna watched John's hand. Unconsciously he reached up to twirl his hair around his finger, as he did when he was moved or agitated.

"Well," answered John, "all the men wear white or blue shirts and suitcoats. And the ladies all wear long, plain cape dresses, made about the same way, and nicely sized Mennonite coverings. Everybody looks about the same."

"And you have a question about that?"

"I don't know," said John. "What do you think?"

"Are you wondering if they live in a 'box,' as people say?" asked Edna.

"Yes, I guess. Are they following form, or are they really serving God? We don't want legalism again.

"He did say the families are training their children. He was impressed with how respectful and in control they were."

"So where are we going on Sunday, John?" Edna lifted questioning eyes to her husband's face.

"For my part, I'm not interested in Living Waters," said John. "Churches that try to operate on what people perceive to be the leading of the Spirit almost always follow a downward course. They tend to fall into an emotional-response pattern that interprets the Bible to fit with their desired position. And instead of the Spirit's leading, it often ends up that they follow their emotions. Our emotions are too fickle to base decisions on." John raised his eyebrows. "Do you want to visit there, Edna?"

"No, I don't think so. I agree with you. I want to focus on the Bible, with an application that has been a blessing. I'm not trying to be liberal. I just want to be alive to God and lead a holy life that honors Him. Jesus said that if we love Him, we will obey Him."

John nodded. "Yes. I know exactly what you mean. Like James said, the form we follow must issue from the contents of our hearts. A religion that doesn't come out in the daily life of the believer will mean nothing when we die.

"This is what I'm thinking. We could go to Meadow Brook for several Sundays; and then if we want to, we can visit Pine Ridge too. Would you be happy with that?"

"I know you have been seeking God. And if that's what you think we should do, I'm happy with that," Edna answered. "But what do Mennonites believe about headship?"

"They believe that everyone is responsible to God to do what is right. They teach that man should be the leader, while his wife is submissive to him."

"How is that different from the way the group believes at Living Waters?" asked Edna.

"Well, I'm not quite sure," answered John. "I think they both believe largely the same thing. Abner said he asked the men from Living Waters about their headship position when they visited after lunch. He said they place accountability a little differently from what the Mennonites do. The men said they tell a woman not to wear a covering if her husband doesn't want her to—and that the husband will bear the blame for the decision instead of his wife. They focus more on the wife's being responsible to God through her husband. The Mennonites are clear that the wife should always obey Bible teachings, with more focus on being directly responsible to God for her soul."

Edna nodded. "I begin to see what you mean," she said. "I'm glad to be submissive to you, John. But do you think I should ever do anything wrong to please you?"

"No," answered John. "The Bible says that we should obey God rather than man."

Edna looked up as the clock struck nine. The evening had passed so quickly!

"When do you want to get a car, Edna?" asked John.

"What are you thinking, John?"

"I'd say not until we know for sure that we're joining another church. Do you mind waiting that long?"

Edna smiled. "No, we've made out fine with a horse and buggy all our lives. So I'm not in a hurry. Maybe waiting for a while will make it just a little easier for my parents too," she added as an afterthought.

"And now let's move toward going to bed," yawned

John. "I can already hear that rooster crowing in my mind."

Edna smiled. "One more decision. What kind of tea do you want?"

John laughed softy, to avoid waking the children. "Anything, Edna. Those kinds of decisions don't matter. But do we have something relaxing?"

"Yes," she answered, quietly joining his laughter. Rising, she reached for the sewing basket on the table and placed the last unfinished sock inside. She opened the cupboard door. "I'll get chamomile tea for you," she finished.

CHAPTER 6

Friday morning rolled around with heaps of soiled clothing. Edna put the last load into the washing machine and started the agitator.

"Somebody is here!" called Rachel.

Leaving the washhouse, Edna hurried to the house door. It was Mrs. Morris, an egg customer.

"Any eggs today?" she queried.

"I have a few," said Edna. "But not more than two dozen."

"I'll take those." Mrs. Morris placed money in Edna's hand and accepted the egg cartons. She headed toward the door, but at the door she hesitated.

"Can I help you with something else?" Edna asked.

"Uh, yes. Do you mind if I ask you some questions about your religion?"

"That's fine," Edna said with a warm smile.

"I really admire you plain people for your way of life,"

Mrs. Morris began. "But I don't know much about you. What do you believe?"

"I believe that God wants me to know Him personally," Edna began, "and that the blood of Jesus is the only way we can be redeemed from the curse of sin that is in every heart."

"Don't I know!" Mrs. Morris exclaimed. "There is so much wickedness all around now. It's hardly safe to turn on the TV anymore."

"We also believe that the Bible is God's message for us, and in it God teaches us how to live." Edna paused and then continued. "I want to live to please God because I love Him."

"Wonderful!" exclaimed Mrs. Morris, "I wish everyone would because then the world would be a better place."

"May I ask if you are a believer, Mrs. Morris?"

"Well now, that's a good question." Mrs. Morris hesitated and drew in her breath sharply. "Am I a believer? I believe there is a God, and I have been reading my Bible. But I guess I don't really believe, or I would live differently. I know I shouldn't smoke, and then there is my marriage, . . ." she finished lamely.

"Yes?" Edna queried.

"Uh," Mrs. Morris began. "Uh, I'm divorced and remarried. Does the Bible say that is wrong?"

"It does. Would you like to look at the Bible with me?"

"No, not now," Mrs. Morris answered, "because I have been reading those verses myself. I was wondering what you people say about that. Most churches today don't pay attention to those verses. They say that it's all right to divorce and remarry as long as you forgive each other." She fidgeted nervously with her pocketbook. "But in my heart I know that doesn't sound right," she finished quietly.

"I'll be praying for you," Edna promised.

She watched as Mrs. Morris's Cadillac drove slowly out the lane. Then Edna hurried back to finish her laundry. Lifting the wash basket, she headed to the back yard. But her thoughts were far from the clothespins and wet wash her nimble fingers touched as they flew from one garment to the next.

So many people knew little about real Christianity. Too many, like wealthy Mrs. Morris, looked enviously at the peace of a simple dedication to Christ but were afraid to make a radical commitment.

"Mama," asked Rachel, "what did Mrs. Morris want?"

"She wanted to talk about God."

"Doesn't she know about God?" Rachel was puzzled.

"She does a little," Edna replied. "But she probably never had a father and mother who taught her about Him."

"But you did, didn't you?"

"Yes," Edna answered hesitantly. For a moment, she pondered her answer. Had her parents really taught her about the God that she had recently come to know personally? Into her mind flashed a picture of Father reading Bible stories to the family on Sunday evenings, of her mother singing hymns while she worked, and of going to church where the Word of God was read. Her parents had taught her to be disciplined and to have respect for authority. Those things had all helped to shape her spirit to the point where she had been ready to make a complete commitment.

"Yes, Rachel," Edna continued, looking down into Rachel's blue eyes. "Grandma and Grandpa read us Bible stories, and they taught and trained me to honor God."

Long after Rachel had run off to play with Paul in the sandbox, Edna savored the answer she had given Rachel. She smiled. Yes, her parents had taught her about God! To be honest about that question freed something in her spirit. For in the pain of feeling rejected as she and John were leaving Shady Glen, the opportunity to become bitter against them was never far away. But even in the deep grief of her spirit, she could not lock her heart against them. They had taught her about God and had done many things to be worthy parents. She would always remember that and be grateful. Perhaps sometime they would understand. And in the meantime, she would be a faithful, honorable daughter.

Later, as she and John finished the evening chores together, Edna shared about the day. She told John about the conversation she had had with Mrs. Morris, Rachel's question, and the thought trains her mind had followed afterward.

John listened quietly. He nodded and then ventured, "We have inner freedom when we are honest about what is true.

"You were honest about the good training you received, rather than throwing up a wall of resentment against your family. We also know your parents will shun us. Both issues are true. You have been fortunate to be in a home where your parents taught you about the Bible and to respect God.

It is also true that our relationship with them will become strained because of our decision and their response to it. But we must refuse to respond carnally. We can't become defensive against them or fail to acknowledge the good they have brought into our lives. You can keep your past and the blessings it has brought to you. That is a gift from your family that you can keep."

After a pause, John said softly, "You realize that even though we withdrew our membership, this is the Sunday for us to be put under the ban, the same as if we were excommunicated. Are you ready for that?"

"No," answered Edna, "I don't suppose I ever will be. You know what the ban and excommunication mean to people who have been part of a close community all their lives. We will lose family closeness and the blessing and approval of many of the people we have grown up with, who have been our friends. And we won't have the security of belonging like we used to."

"A lot of them won't wave to us when they meet us on the road, and they will avoid us in town," John added. "That will be difficult for me because friends and their acceptance mean a lot to me. But I plan to remind myself that God's acceptance of me is not affected by what people do." He lifted his hat and began to twirl the hair at the back of his head. "Sometimes we think God looks at us the same way people look at us. But that's another one of those carnal mindsets that drives us in circles. Following truth will make us free, indeed!"

"I'm trying to look squarely at everything," Edna continued, "and believe what is true about God. Then I can be honest about what really *is*."

"Yes," said John. "When we do that, we'll be ready to do the next right thing, without picking up burdens that weigh us down."

"What I really will miss is the full blessing of my parents," Edna said as tears sprang to her eyes.

"I know," John said, squeezing her hand. "That is a real loss because that is one of the real heart treasures of life. But God's children can claim this verse: 'When my father and my mother forsake me, then the LORD will take me up.' Do you feel that you really have lost your mother's blessing?"

"Well, no," answered Edna, "not really. She is troubled about our leaving. But her heart will still be turned toward me with love and care and, I think, a measure of her blessing. But she will need to honor what Father wants her to do in relation to us."

"And it's right that she would," John said seriously, "because Father is her husband. I'm sure she feels that she is in a difficult spot."

"Yes," said Edna. "She as much as said that. I know Father still cares about us. He is carrying his pain in such a hard way that his eyes look dull. It hurts me so much to see him. He just does not understand. Do you think he ever will, John?"

"I don't know. But I know you will be a faithful daughter, and we will ask God to open up ways for us to bless him."

"And Mother and I will pray for each other every morning," Edna said softly as a tender smile softened the seriousness on her face. "That feels like a lifeline to me!"

CHAPTER 7

John lifted his Bible from the bookshelf and sat down in the rocking chair. The Bible fell open to John 15. His eyes were drawn to verse 5. "I am the vine, ye are the branches: He that abideth in me, and I in him, the same bringeth forth much fruit: for without me ye can do nothing."

"Lord," prayed John, "without You, I can do nothing. Nothing! Move in my life so that I will be a faithful follower. Teach us to worship You and honor You. Flow with Your life into my branch so that I will be fruitful. It is the only way."

John was on his knees when Edna entered the kitchen thirty minutes later. Edna moved quietly about the kitchen as she prepared breakfast. She looked up as the stair door opened. It was Rachel.

"Good morning, Rachel." Edna smiled as she stooped to kiss the little girl. "Did you sleep well last night?"

Rachel nodded and walked over to John's rocking chair.

"Daddy," Rachel asked as John rose from his knees, "can you hold me?"

"Yes," John answered. Sitting in the chair again, he reached for the little girl and began rocking her. Rachel laid her head against his shoulder and looked up into his face.

"I always feel safe when you hold me," she said, smiling.

"Is that a nice way to wake up?"

"Umm-huh." Rachel nodded.

Edna looked over at the pair, and her eyes met John's. He smiled tenderly as if he read her thoughts. How much she also needed her heavenly Father to hold her.

"Lord," Edna prayed silently, "I can be safe only when You're holding me. Be with us today as we go to Meadow Brook for the first time."

"Well," said John as he finished his oatmeal, "it's going to take us half an hour to drive over to Meadow Brook. Can you be ready by eight-fifteen?"

"I'll try," said Edna. "I should wake up Hannah anyway. Can you dress Paul?"

It was beginning to drizzle as they drove out the lane. "This will be different," said John. "We hardly know what other churches are like. I'll be praying for you, Edna," he added. "May the Lord prepare our hearts and give us a blessing."

"I know how you feel," answered Edna. "I'm sort of scared—and excited—at the same time."

The parking lot was beginning to fill as they entered the churchyard. John guided Lady to a large tree and tied her with the lead rope. Turning to the buggy, he helped Edna with the children.

"Good morning." A short, balding man approached the buggy, walking with a decided limp. "I'm Edward Miller. We're glad you came this morning."

John stepped forward and shook hands. "Good morning," he answered. "I am John Troyer, and this is my wife, Edna," he added, motioning toward Edna.

Edna also shook hands with Edward. His eyes were kind and understanding. A person could feel safe with this man. She turned to meet Edward's wife.

"Everybody calls me Betty," she said as she greeted Edna warmly. "God bless you. We're so glad you're here."

Betty looked at the children. "Our children start going to Sunday school when they are four. Would your little girl like to go? I'll be teaching that class."

Edna looked questioningly at John.

"Rachel is four," John answered, "but I think we'll just keep her with us this morning."

Betty nodded. "That's fine."

John and Edna met several more couples.

"Would you like to sit with me?" Ruth Miller asked as she cradled her own baby. "I usually sit toward the back. Our nursery is back there," she said, pointing to a door at the back of the auditorium.

Edna nodded and followed Ruth to one of the back benches, with Rachel in tow.

The congregation sang heartily as the service began, and music filled every inch of the auditorium. Edna listened attentively during the Sunday school period. She was glad when Hannah fell asleep. What a blessing it would be to really focus on the message.

Edward Miller stood up to preach. He surveyed the congregation kindly. "This morning I am going to share something that is dear to my heart," Brother Edward began. "My title is 'Living the Consecrated Life.' To live a consecrated life, or one that is set apart for God, we must be wholly given to God. The Spirit of God must work His work in us."

John drank in every word of the message. The words fell like rain on his thirsty soul. His pen moved rapidly as he took notes. The congregation listened with rapt attention.

After the message, Brother Edward opened the floor to the congregation. "Is there a testimony, a confession, or a thought you would like to share?"

Edna watched as three brethren stood to share insights from the message. Then a sister confessed a need in her life. The service ended with a closing song and a prayer.

Edna smiled as one lady after another came to meet her. Some were young mothers like herself. Several were gray-haired women.

"We are so glad to have you here," Judith Kauffman said when she met Edna. "We would like to invite you to our house for dinner today."

"Thank you," returned Edna. "I'll ask my husband."

Later, as they headed toward the Kauffman home, John and Edna shared impressions.

"Well, John," said Edna, "what did you think?"

"I was blessed," answered John. "I think I would like to learn more about this congregation. How about you?"

"I agree with you," said Edna.

When they pulled into the Kauffman farm lane, several cars John had seen at church were already there.

"Oh!" exclaimed Edna. "I see Edward and Betty's car. It will be nice to have them here. Who did you say the other minister is?"

"Edward is the bishop," John answered, "and Steve Kauffman, who lives here, is a minister. I met the deacon too. His name is Moses Good."

Edna busied herself helping the children as Steve Kauffman approached John's side of the surrey.

"I'll put your horse in the barn," he offered. "I have an empty stall. This used to be an Amish farm." He turned to Edna. "You are welcome to go to the house while we stable the horse. Judith is waiting for you at the door."

As Edna entered the kitchen, she smiled to see that Ruth Miller was already cutting bread and Betty setting the table.

The conversation flowed pleasantly at the table. Edna savored the food. These ladies certainly were not lacking any cooking skills.

"Did you know, Edna," Betty began as the women settled in the dining room to visit after lunch, "that Edward and I used to be Old Order Amish?"

"No," Edna answered, "I didn't."

"My parents were Old Older Mennonites," said Judith. "But I don't remember that, because I was only two when they changed churches."

"I can imagine this could be a difficult day for you," Betty continued. "Did I hear John tell Edward that this is the first time you are visiting another church?"

"Yes." Edna nodded. "Today our names were to be removed from the church membership at Shady Glen. When John visited our bishop, Sam Troyer, to tell him we were removing our membership, he said that we would be put under the ban today."

"Oh, I'm sorry!" Betty spoke with feeling. "That happened years ago for us, but I remember exactly how it felt. To lose the security of a close church circle and to step out to make a new life with other people takes a lot of courage."

"Well," said Edna, "it is hard. But we just want to do the right thing."

Judith nodded. "I'm sure you do. How do your families feel about this?"

"John's parents understand," Edna began, "but my family will shun us. That is very hard for me," she finished as she wiped a tear from her eye.

"Now the Lord will raise up other people to be your family." Ruth squeezed Edna's hand warmly. "When we give up something for God, He always gives us something else that meets our needs."

"Yes," said Judith. "Sometimes God provides through other people, and sometimes He just gives us more of Himself."

"Remember this," Betty suggested. "When you feel rejected by your old friends and family, don't take it personally. Refuse to grow bitter. Share love; then your heart will be free."

Edna nodded and pondered the thoughts. Mentally she stowed them away in her heart—like treasured jewels.

Judith's older girls took all the children outside to play. The afternoon passed rapidly as they continued visiting.

Toward evening, John appeared in the doorway. "Are you ready, Edna?"

Edna nodded and stood up to collect the children's things.

"Edna, we were glad to visit with you and John." Brother Edward smiled kindly. "And we welcome you to Meadow Brook anytime." He turned to John. "Seek God's will, and He will be faithful in leading you. We will be praying for you."

"Well," said John as he pulled onto the road, "I think we are making new friends, aren't we, Edna?"

"Yes," said Edna, "and I have an idea we will need them very soon. Have you been remembering the announcement Bishop Sam was going to make this morning?"

"I sure have," John answered with a pained look on his face. "But now we must go on—on to the next step."

A surrey approached them on the road. "Jerry Miller's," John said softly to Edna. As they passed each other, John lifted his hand. "Hello!" he said pleasantly.

Edna felt her stomach twist into a knot as Jerry and his wife looked straight ahead, as if she and John were not there. But their faces looked extremely uncomfortable. Only four-year-old Jeremy, in the back seat, waved.

"The poor people!" John said after they had passed. "Did you notice their expressions?"

"Yes," said Edna. "I did." She paused. "So this is what it means to be shunned."

"I'm sorry, Edna," John said tenderly. "It is."

Chapter 8

"Come, children," Edna called. "The mailman just came. Let's walk out the lane and see what surprise is waiting for us in the mailbox."

Rachel and Paul came running.

"Can I pull Hannah in the wagon?" asked Rachel.

"Me puth!" Paul shouted.

"Or better yet," said Edna, "we'll put you all into the wagon. Rachel, you hold Hannah, and Paul can sit in the back."

Lady galloped over to the fence and neighed. Edna patted her nose. "Good girl, Lady!" she said.

Edna looked about her. Fall was beginning to whisper in the air. The garden was turning a bit yellow—with the forsaken look of spent crops. A V of geese flew overhead.

"Honkerth, Mama!" squealed Paul.

"Yes, Paul," Edna said. "God tells the geese when they should fly south because cold weather will be coming.

After a while we will need to wear our warm coats again, and snow will fall on the ground."

Edna stopped as they reached the end of the lane. She opened the mailbox and pulled out the mail. "Oh!" she exclaimed as she put a handful of junk mail into the wagon. "We have a letter from Grandma!"

Edna's heart beat with excitement as she hurried in the lane again. Sitting in her rocker, she tore open the letter.

"Dear Edna," the letter read, "I hope you and the children are having a beautiful day. I think of you so much, and I am still praying for you every morning. Are you still praying for me then too? I pray for you at six-fifteen when I am having my devotions—and of course, many other times because you are always in my thoughts.

"Father said that he doesn't want you to come to see us, but he doesn't care if we write to each other. So I am glad we can do that. I will write to you every week, like I write to the other married children who live away from here. And if you have time to write back to me, I can still hear about what is happening to you and John and the cute things the children are doing.

"I am praying that God will keep you faithful as you are making important decisions. Stay free from the world."

Edna wiped tears of joy as she finished reading about the small happenings at her parents' home.

"Thank You, God!" she whispered. "Thank You that I still have my mother. Be with my father and bring him to know You." Edna hurried through her work so that she would have time to write a return letter before supper.

"Come, Rachel and Paul," Edna called as she collected

writing supplies. "Would you like to draw some pictures for Grandpa and Grandma?"

"Yes!" Rachel exclaimed, grabbing her crayons from the shelf. "I will draw a butterfly."

Edna lifted Paul onto a chair and watched him scribble across his clean sheet of paper, only partly guessing the joy the little missive would bring to his grandparents.

Ruth Miller was at the door to meet Edna on Sunday morning. "We're glad you decided to come again," she said as she greeted Edna. "How has this week been?"

Edna hesitated. "A little rough," she answered at last.

"I'd love to hear about it after the service," Ruth said warmly. "Right now I'm headed to the nursery to give this little fellow a complete changeover," she added, smiling at the three-month-old baby in her arms.

"I'm looking forward to sharing with you," Edna answered.

Edna sat down and looked at the congregation around her. Friendly, warm faces and loving acceptance welcomed her. So different from the forlorn feeling that had swept over her at the grocery store that week. She had first met Ada Troyer, who had abruptly turned and headed the other direction. And then outside, Thelma had deliberately avoided her on the street, by quickly crossing and walking on the other side. There had been tears in Thelma's eyes in the brief glance they had shared. Worst of all had been meeting her own father on the road, and he had stared coldly ahead, refusing to wave or speak.

Edna drank in the warmth of the service. After Sunday

school, Brother Moses led the congregation in a devotional from Psalm 23. "God will always be with us," he said. "The Good Shepherd will never forsake His sheep. There is never a place where He will not be for us. Cast your burdens upon the Lord, and He will sustain you."

Brother Steve's message was titled "Divine Enablement." "Only *you* can block the path to God," he said with feeling. "Sin will keep us from God. When we crucify our flesh and yield every area of our hearts to God, He is free to dwell within us. His presence sanctifies us and allows Him to surround us with horses and chariots of fire."

"Lord," Edna prayed, "keep me free from sin. I know self-pity is sin. And right now I would so much love to pity myself. Don't let it choke me, Lord. Cleanse me with the blood of Jesus."

Edna listened attentively to Brother Steve. "Jesus went through every temptation we face," he said. "He came through blamelessly because He believed and acted upon what God said. What area of your life do you need to commit to God? Give it to Him, and He will bring good from that very thing."

Edna pondered that for a moment. How had Jesus responded when He was mistreated? "My meat is to do the will of him that sent me, and to finish his work," Jesus had said. And that was what He focused on when He hung on the cross.

The small grievances of the week shrank into realistic proportion in Edna's mind. Yes, she and John had been treated rudely. But what was that compared to what Jesus had endured as He was falsely accused, ridiculed, beaten, and finally crucified? And He had gone through it all blamelessly. And here she was, feeling badly because a few people had ignored her. Edna bowed her head in shame.

Brother Steve's words jerked her attention back to the message. "So much lies in our focus," Brother Steve was saying. "Jesus was pure because He always focused on truth. Truth is what God is, what God thinks, and the way God knows situations to be.

"When we operate on the basis of things that are not true, we give Satan a stronghold. That stronghold gives the devil a landing pad in our lives to come in with his 'helicopters' and corrupt us. Then we develop false beliefs and expectations. We think we deserve the best. Our feelings become very important to us. We get hung up until other people treat us right. We must have our own way. We are sure we are always right.

"We must remain humble and focused on God, or we will allow Satan to build these strongholds in our lives. Pride and self-pity will finally bind us hand and foot and take us away from the God we first loved."

Suddenly, pouring all the hurt feelings of the week into Ruth's sympathetic ears lost its appeal. Instead Edna determined to share the goodness of God in bringing her back from her self-pity trip to focusing on God and obeying Him.

"I'm sorry, Lord," Edna prayed. "Thank You for bringing my eyes back to You."

A quiet peace filled her heart as she listened to the remainder of the message.

"I'm sorry about your week," Ruth said after the service.

Edna smiled and laughed softly. "After hearing the message this morning, I don't have much to say. A few people were rude to me. But what is that?

"God made me aware of my smallness this morning and brought my attention back to Him. I'll just ask you to pray for me that God will not allow me to pity myself. Then God can bring good from these situations," Edna finished. "Will you do that?"

"I surely will," Ruth said with feeling. "And I have confessed my resentment against my sister-in-law to God. Will you pray for me?"

A few more Sundays passed. John stood at the back of the congregation, walking Hannah, who was more fussy than normal because of teething. For a few moments, John's eyes surveyed the congregation. His brow furrowed slightly. This was the third Sunday he had seen Andrew Zimmerman's children communicating and laughing during church, when they should have been listening to the sermon. And what about the two teenagers who slouched on the back bench, chewing gum? Did they really come to worship God? Why did the Zimmerman family generally stay in a close circle with a few friends who also appeared to be less than dedicated?

"Can you come for dinner today?" Moses Good invited after church. "You've been coming here long enough that you might have a few questions. We're not having anyone else, so it would be a good time to get acquainted and discuss anything you would like to talk about."

John smiled. "We'll come. I was just thinking of a few

questions I would like to ask."

Edna felt very much at home in the simple surroundings of Moses and Sally's home. Sally was quiet but reached out from the true warmth of her heart.

"Thank you so much for the casserole you dropped off last Thursday," Edna said. "It came just at the right time, when I longed to have a friend drop in. I don't see how you manage to do everything you do. How long has your husband been ordained?"

Sally smiled. "That was seven years ago, just after our second child was born," she replied. "It changed a lot of things in our lives. But then what do we want more than being busy for God?"

Edna nodded. Sally certainly was busy with six children and many other activities. When the congregation needed them, Moses and Sally were there.

"And now for those questions," Moses said, when the dishes were done and Sally and Edna had seated themselves in the living room. "I guess you know that our congregation—and the other two churches where Brother Edward is bishop—are independent churches. On occasion Brother Edward will confer with other bishops from churches we have a loose association with."

John nodded.

"You've been here with us long enough to see that we're imperfect," Moses continued. "Maybe you're wondering about some things or about the way we handle situations in our congregation."

John pondered quietly before he spoke. "Yes," he said, "I do have a few questions. I'm not expecting any church to be perfect. What we want is a stable church that is heading in the right direction, with Jesus Christ at the center.

"But I have been wondering about some of the young people who seem careless and indifferent. Especially those two boys who sit on the back seat together most Sundays."

"Yes. You're talking about Howard Hoover and Vernon Zimmerman." Moses nodded. "What did you notice?"

"Well," answered John, "I noticed they slouch and chew gum in church. Their hair is long and stylish, and the clothes they wear give the appearance of ones who are trying to flirt with the world—hardly in line with the discipline. The general impression I get when I see them is that they are trying to fill a vacuum that needs to be filled with God. Or maybe they aren't church members?"

"Yes," Moses said slowly. "They are church members. I understand the concerns you have because I carry the same burden for them. Go on."

"Something seems less than dedicated about the Zimmerman family. Am I being too critical?"

"No," Moses answered seriously. "Your eyes are open, and you are seeing problems that do exist. Most of our congregation are concerned, spiritual families who are trying to do the right thing. But we do have some people that concern us. We are praying that God will work in the hearts of the young people and the family you talked about. They do tend to run close to the edge of our guidelines for godly living."

"Is there a reason, like sickness, that the Zimmermans frequently miss Wednesday evening services?" asked John.

Moses sighed. "No. That has to do with work. Andrew

is a gifted businessman. But sometimes he is still out on the job when it's time to leave for church, and his wife doesn't like to come without him.

"Materialism," Moses said quietly. "The cares of life and a love for riches can choke out the love of God in our hearts. Why don't you share some of your questions with Brother Edward too?"

"Maybe I should," John answered. "Shall we drop in at their place on the way home, Edna?"

"Sure, if you want to," Edna replied.

Edna smiled as they walked into the warmth of Brother Edward's home.

"Good afternoon," Brother Edward said as he shook John's hand. "We're glad you came. Betty and I were just talking about coming over to see you this evening."

"We are just on the way home from Brother Moses' place," John began after a bit of chitchat. "We were discussing some things, and he recommended that I discuss them with you."

"We're glad to talk anytime," Brother Edward offered. "What is it?"

"Edna and I feel welcome, and we are being fed spiritually as we share with the congregation at Meadow Brook. We are very grateful for the way you have received us. However, we have a few questions.

"I notice that a few of the young people seem to be unconcerned about spiritual things, and they barely fit into the discipline. And some things about the Zimmerman family raise questions in my mind. Do you know what I mean?"

"I do." Brother Edward nodded. "You have a right to ask these questions and to know how we handle things. Betty and I are concerned to see indifference in the church family too. I am praying that hearts will be changed and that each person will want to do right from the heart. We are teaching, admonishing, and reaching out to encourage the weaker members. So we are working on the problem. But we need to give the Spirit of God more time to work in their hearts."

John nodded and turned to another subject. "We really appreciate the messages we are hearing and the spiritual fellowship we find with most of the families. That means more than you can know, since we have lost most of the friendships we used to have."

"Forty years ago we were in the same place you are now," Brother Edward responded warmly. "We know how it feels to make new beginnings. But I think we are the ones who are blessed by having you here. Your testimony encourages us."

"We just want to do the right thing and honor God," John replied quietly.

"What do you think, John?" Edna asked as they traveled home.

"About Brother Edward's explanation of the way they are handling people with spiritual problems?"

"Yes."

"I'm trying to sort things out," John replied. "He recognizes the problem and seems concerned. And it is Biblical that we teach and encourage one another when there are 'weaker brothers.' But I'm not sure about the issue of giving them time. I guess that depends on how much time you give a person before you use discipline when they have a spiritual problem. I would certainly think that a spiritual man like Brother Edward would deal with sin."

"I hope so," Edna said. "Do you think we should check out Pine Ridge while we're making our decision?"

"Yes," John returned. "We should. Let's go there a few times and learn to know them too. I'll ask James which weeks they have prayer meeting. We could start this Wednesday, if prayer meeting is scheduled for this week."

CHAPTER 9

Edna hurried out to the kitchen to wash the dinner dishes. James would be picking them up at 7:00 to go to prayer meeting at Pine Ridge, and quite a few things had to be done before that.

Edna breathed a sigh of relief as she settled into the back seat of James's car that evening. In twenty minutes, they pulled into the parking lot.

"Welcome!" James smiled as he opened his car door. "We are glad to have you."

Edna entered yet another church with a little trepidation. Rose Miller stepped forward to meet her at the door. "We are so glad to have you, Edna," she said as she pressed Edna's hand warmly. "I'm Rose Miller. James has been telling us about the little group he used to have Bible studies with, and we have been praying for all of you."

Edna looked into the aging face and noted the eyes that shone warmly from the mother heart inside. "Thank you, Rose!" she said. "We surely appreciate that. Our new friends and their spiritual concern for us means so much to us while we make decisions that will shape our lives."

Three more sisters were waiting to meet Edna.

"I'm Denise Horst," a blue-eyed young lady said, smiling. "And these are my children, David and Angela. We've been praying for you, and we're so glad you came to worship with us."

"I'm glad to meet you," Edna returned. "Is that your husband talking to my husband?"

"No," Denise answered quietly. "My husband passed away . . . last year."

"Oh, I'm sorry," Edna ventured. "I didn't know."

"That's all right. I don't mind talking about it, if you don't mind if I cry a little."

"Not at all," Edna said. "I don't know what that would be like. I'll be praying for you too."

The service was warm and heart filling. Edna joined heartily in the singing. A man who was introduced as Brother Aaron had devotions on the goodness of God. Then prayer requests were taken, and the group split into little groups to pray. Edna enjoyed the time of close sharing with the six sisters in her group.

"Do you still want to come next Sunday morning?" James asked as they got out of the car at home.

"Yes," John answered. "We decided we'll go to all your services for a two-week period."

"All right." James smiled. "I'll pick you up at eight-thirty on Sunday morning."

Edna listened attentively on Sunday morning. The superintendent's Sunday school devotions from Psalm 46 brought courage to her spirit. "We serve a mighty God!" Levi Mast said fervently. "When we look to Him in our trouble, He hears us and makes a way for us. When we go wrong, He uses His staff to bring correction or to redirect us. God is always ready to hear the repentant heart and to bring us back to obedience and fellowship with Him. God will move mountains for us when we trust Him. We will always have God. Therefore, we are always safe."

Edna cataloged the thoughts for further reference, to use later that week. "Lord," she prayed, "I want to obey You in everything. Teach me to do Your will."

Brother Wilmer Peachy brought the message. "Today," he said, "I have the privilege of bringing a message on consecration. The world has nothing to offer us. Anything the devil offers us will end in a curse. But with God, there is always blessing upon blessing.

"Today we are going to look at 'Being Separate From the World.' What a joy to be a part of the kingdom of God! As children of God, we are a part of a kingdom that begins here and continues through eternity."

Edna listened attentively to the six points of the message. Peace filled her heart. How good to hear solid convictions preached earnestly!

The second Sunday morning the family attended at Pine Ridge, John approached Edna after church. "We're invited to Aaron Miller's for dinner today," he said. "Has anyone else asked you if we can come?"

"No," Edna replied. "They have a host schedule like

they do at Meadow Brook. So everyone knows who is responsible for visitors."

"Good. Then I'll tell Aaron we can come. James is invited too."

Rose Miller's dinner was delicious. Edna smiled as she looked around the table and counted the blessings of friendship with each one. James and his carload stayed for a while after the others left.

"Well," Brother Aaron said with a smile, "is there any way we can help you as you choose a path for the future?"

"For one thing," answered John, "please pray for us. I know your whole congregation already has been, and we appreciate that tremendously.

"As I look about your congregation, I noticed very few people who are obviously fence pushers. Is your whole congregation committed to what your church stands for?"

"Well," Brother Aaron replied, "sometimes issues that need to be addressed come up in our members' lives. You won't find us a perfect church. Right now we have a young man who needs to make a decision. He will need to decide if he wants to remove carnality and spiritual indifference from his life or forfeit his membership. We will give him time to make a decision, while we work with him. But he will have to make a decision.

"God calls us to choose between good and evil. He hates lukewarmness, and little foxes that come in spoil the vine. We try to keep current and deal with issues as we go along and do not allow carnal members to retain their membership. We try to keep the lines clear so our people will know what our expected standard is. God says, 'Be ye holy; for I am holy.' "

John leaned forward and began twirling his hair with his finger. "Do you feel that drawing the lines that firmly tends to bring legalism?"

"That's an honest question," Brother Aaron returned. "And coming from your background, I can see why you wonder. It is possible for someone to look fairly good and yet lack salvation—because they are simply following form. To serve God, we must have heart content that issues outward in a godly form, or culture. *Culture* simply means the way we do things. Every person has a culture that he follows.

"Our Christianity is worth nothing if the Spirit of God does not live in our hearts. If humility and an open attitude toward God and His authorities are lacking, we know that God is not reigning in that heart. So, a man who says he loves God but lives for the world has a religion that is nothing but an empty profession.

"Heart content and form cannot be separated, any more than you can decide if it is better to have front tires or back tires on your car."

John chuckled. "Well, no, I guess you're right. I'd hate to try to go somewhere in a two-wheeled car."

"You wouldn't get very far," James said with a smile.

"A spiritual, disciplined church is a church at rest, one that is ready to go forward to do the work of God. You are used to horses. How much work could you get done with a team that is always kicking and refusing to go the way the driver wants them to go?"

"Not much, for sure!" John responded.

"It's the same in church life," Brother Aaron continued. "A church can be a source of strength to its members and a witness in the community when lives have been cleansed by God and submitted to Him in obedience. Then there is no chafing against God. Jesus said, 'Ye are my friends, if ye do whatsoever I command you.' "

Brother Aaron thought for a moment. "Another source of strength to our church is our larger fellowship," he continued. "We have close ties with other churches in our fellowship, and that provides a mutual strength for all of us. The bishops who have responsibility in our sister churches are ready to help with needs in each other's churches as well. We value that blessing."

"I can see the wisdom of that," John said, nodding thoughtfully. "Thank you for sharing."

James pushed his chair back from the table and stretched his legs out comfortably. He had just eaten supper with John and Edna, and he looked at them now across the table. "I'm about ready to ask for church membership at Pine Ridge," he said. "Do you feel I'm making the right decision, John?"

"I have no problem with that," said John. "If that's where God is leading you, we wish you God's blessing." He paused a moment. Then he asked, "Do you have a Pine Ridge church standard of discipline along? I'd like to compare that with Meadow Brook's standard."

"I think I do in the car. I'll be back in," James said as he quickly rose to his feet.

Edna sat beside John as the two men compared the

requirements for the two congregations.

At last John closed the little booklet in his hand. "Both churches require plain, modest dress, separation from the world, and no radios or TVs," he said thoughtfully. "There's not a great difference between the two standards, though Pine Ridge has a few points Meadow Brook doesn't have."

"From my observation," said James, "I believe Pine Ridge is probably stricter in enforcing their discipline than Meadow Brook is."

"I know," said John, "and I don't know quite what to think. I feel spiritual life at both places, and I enjoy worshiping and sharing in each congregation. But the same strictness that produces the uniformity at Pine Ridge makes me feel a little stifled, when I want the freedom of following God's Spirit."

Edna jumped up as a knock sounded on the door.

"Why, come in, Abner and Emma!" she exclaimed.

"If it isn't our old prayer meeting group!" John said, smiling. "Come in."

Laughter and pleasant conversation filled the living room, and the evening passed quickly.

"Shall we have a time of sharing and prayer before we leave?" Abner asked.

"Yes," said John. "You were our leader before. Go ahead, Abner."

"Then suppose we each share where we are in our decisions and any concerns we would like the group to remember in prayer," Abner suggested. "And then we could all pray together."

"I'll start. We are really being blessed," Abner began.

"We're still attending at Living Waters. There are a few things we've had to get used to. But over all, we are very happy where we are and are growing in the Lord. We are learning that our spiritual security lies in what Christ has done for us, rather than in what we do. All our righteousness is as filthy rags. Pray for us that we will be faithful in following the Lord."

"I'm still going to Pine Ridge, as you probably all know," James began. "I am ready to apply for membership. I appreciate the spiritual life and stability I find there. Please pray for me that I will follow Christ faithfully and do His will. That is the deepest desire of my heart."

"We're not quite sure what we're going to do," John said slowly. "But we're at the point of deciding to go either to Meadow Brook or Pine Ridge. We want a spiritual, consistent church that puts God first. Please pray for us that God will show us clearly what He wants us to do."

"Lord," Edna prayed silently as the group knelt, "bless each one here. Teach us all to do Your will. Keep us safe spiritually and provide influences that will help our children to love and honor You."

Edna rose from her knees refreshed. But something troubled her when she looked into Emma's eyes. Some of the joy was gone.

"I'll be praying for you, Emma," Edna whispered as Emma moved toward the door.

"Thank you," said Emma as she quickly wiped away a tear. "I'll be counting on that."

And then they were gone, leaving question marks in the air.

"What kind of tea do you want, John?" Edna asked after the children were in bed.

"Just some good mint, please," answered John. Then he sat deep in thought, quietly staring ahead.

"Deep thoughts?" questioned Edna as she brought the tea to the table and sat down beside her husband.

"Yes," John answered. "Our two weeks of attending at Pine Ridge are over, and now we need to decide which way we will go."

Edna nodded. "What do you think, John? I've been praying that God will give you wisdom."

"What would you like to do, Edna?"

"Well," Edna answered, "I have been fed spiritually both places, and I have friends in both congregations. In one sense, I feel a little more like I fit at Pine Ridge."

"I know what you mean," John said. "We're planning to stay conservative, and the lines are clear there. That brings rest." He paused a moment and then said slowly, "My question is whether Pine Ridge has the spiritual freedom we are looking for. I like what I see there, and yet I wonder . . . Are they a little too rigid? I'm going to fast for three days to seek God's will. I'll take off from work on Thursday and Friday. Then we can make our decision after that."

For a few minutes, the couple sat in silence. The only sound was the tinkle of Edna's spoon tapping her cup.

"You're smiling, Edna," John said, looking at her. "It looks as if you're thinking a happy, tender thought."

Edna laughed. "Well, maybe I was, John. It really isn't any of my business, but I'm wondering if James will see what a wonderful person Denise Horst is."

"Who is that?" John asked, his forehead puckered.

"You probably wouldn't have met her," Edna returned. "She is the young widow at Pine Ridge. Her husband died of cancer a year ago, and she must have grown better instead of bitter through the experience. I just love her."

"James is a good, steady fellow," John said, a little smile pulling at the corners of his lips. "He deserves a good wife." He was silent for a moment.

"What do you think about Abner's?" he asked.

Edna raised her eyebrows questioningly.

"I mean," he continued, "do you think things will work out for them at Living Waters? Pete Miller's and Timothy Esh's both left Old Order churches and went to Living Waters. That was about five years ago, if I remember right. Their families still seem to be principled. I am hoping Abner will do the same thing if they keep going to Living Waters." John paused.

"If any man started out meaning to do the right thing, it was Abner," he continued with feeling. "So many times he has been an inspiration to me in serving God. But I'm beginning to wonder if *wanting* to do the right thing is enough. Did you notice the rapid changes his family is making?"

Edna nodded, with a troubled expression. "Yes, I did, and Emma cried as they were leaving, though she hardly said anything. She gave me an unopened box, John, and I can only guess what's in it. It would be dreadful if one's husband wouldn't hold solid convictions and would pull the family that way."

John nodded solemnly and began to twirl his hair.

CHAPTER 10

Eagerly Edna tore open her mother's weekly letter. This time it had taken two days to arrive.

"What does Grandma's letter say?" asked Rachel. "Did she like the picture I made for her last week?"

Edna smiled and handed a letter to Rachel. "This is your letter from Grandma," she said.

Rachel squealed with delight.

"This is what the letter says," continued Edna. "Dear Rachel, Thank you so much for the picture of your cat that you sent me last week. I really enjoy him! I see him every time I open the refrigerator, because I keep your pictures on the refrigerator door. Love, Grandma."

Rachel hugged the letter and ran off to show it to Paul, while Edna scanned her own.

"Dear daughter," she read. "Greetings in Jesus' Name. You don't know how much pleasure your letters bring to me. I know you are busy. I remember how it was when I was in your place, and yet you take the time to write.

"Father does not want me to share your letters with the children. So I keep them in my dresser drawer, and only Father knows where they are. But I often find the letters in a different order than I left them—or refolded a little differently than I fold them. And there are smudges on the sheets that are not from my tears. So you are writing to both of your parents. We both love you."

Edna hurried to her bedroom, shut the door, and sobbed tears of mingled joy and sadness against her pillow. Father still loved her. He might not acknowledge her when they passed on the road. He might not welcome the family to visit. But in the secrecy of his bedroom, he rummaged through the letters she wrote to her mother and shed tears over the messages from a daughter he loved and missed.

The end of the week approached. Edna tried especially hard to keep the children quiet so they would not disturb John as he fasted and sought God's will. And when she was able to, she joined him in prayer.

"Lord," prayed John, from the quietness of the guest room upstairs, "what do You want us to do? We need Your direction so that we will be in Your will. Give us Your thoughts. Teach us to know Your truth. Which church should we go to? Touch my mind, and help me to know Your will for my family."

On Saturday night after the children were in bed, Edna heard the stair door open. She looked up as John entered the kitchen.

"Shall we pray together now, Edna?" he asked.

Quietly John and Edna knelt together in front of the couch. Half an hour later, they rose from their knees.

Edna waited quietly for John to speak.

"Edna," John said softly, "I see spirituality and Biblical application in both of the congregations we're looking at. You know what I have been thinking. We want a church that is spiritual, conservative, and stable. I have been concerned about legalism at Pine Ridge and wondering if there is too much tolerance at Meadow Brook.

"You know I had another talk with Brother Edward on Wednesday night. He has a real burden for the problems in the congregation at Meadow Brook, and he said they do mean to have a pure church. He repeated that they are working with the problems. Unless you feel otherwise, I believe we should become members at Meadow Brook."

"You've been praying and seeking God's will," responded Edna. "I'm happy with whatever you decide. I know you have godly concerns for our family."

"Then that's what we'll plan to do," said John. "Let's keep on attending at Meadow Brook for two more months before we formally ask for church membership. That way the congregation can learn to know us, and we can be more sure that this is God's will for us. That was what Brother Edward advised." John sighed and relaxed against the couch cushions. "It feels good just to know that we have made a decision. Now we know what to do next."

"I know what you mean," said Edna.

John and Edna fell asleep that night with peaceful hearts.

The next two months flew by rapidly. John and Edna enjoyed the fellowship and involvement with the congregation at Meadow Brook.

"I'm beginning to feel that the brothers and sisters at church really are my family, and I feel so blessed in the services," Edna shared with John one night at the supper table. "Isn't it something the way God provides?"

"It is!" John smiled. "Our life still isn't easy. But Jesus promised that when we seek God and His righteousness first, the other things would be added. And God is doing that.

"You know we've been working hard on getting our drivers' licenses. James is coming to take us in for our tests tomorrow. Are you ready?"

"I believe so," replied Edna. "It really isn't that hard. Did you decide which minivan we'll get?"

"Probably the Astro that Abner found for us," John replied. "James can drop us off at the car lot to pick it up after we have our drivers' licenses."

"I guess it's about time for me to start looking like the Meadow Brook sisters," Edna said. "I think Ruth's covering will fit me. Our heads are shaped about the same way, and it comes on my head nicely. Denise helped me make some adjustments on a dress pattern, and she offered to sew the first one for me. Then we'll see how it fits.

"That sounds good." John nodded.

"Oh!" exclaimed Edna, "I almost forgot to tell you, John. I got another letter from my mother today. She said Father doesn't care if she drops in quietly to see us after the baby comes. And that's only about a month away."

John's smile broadened. "Wonderful!" he exclaimed.

"I'm sure that means a lot to you."

"Judith Kauffman said one of her girls can be our maid for the first week," Edna continued. "Then after that she can come to help me on washdays or if I need help with something in particular."

"I'm glad to hear that," John returned. "You will need help. And I wasn't sure how hard it would be to get a maid, since we can't depend on your sister this time."

"We are happy to announce that Brother John and Sister Edna are requesting church membership," Brother Edward announced. "If anyone has something to share with the ministry, we would like to know shortly. Brother John and Sister Edna have been in our hearts for several months now," he continued, "and they continue to bless us. We are hoping to receive them as members within a few weeks, since they do not have membership with any church presently. It is our prayer that we will also be a blessing to them as they become a part of the congregation."

Edna looked at the congregation around her. How much she would treasure this kind of belonging again! Ruth reached over and squeezed Edna's hand. Edna smiled into Ruth's warm eyes. Ruth was almost like a sister—another of God's provisions.

Helen Steiner came over to meet Edna after the service. "I understand you have lost family," she said simply. "When you want someone to keep the children or to make doughnuts with, remember it would be my pleasure to share that with you. You inspire me so much with your quiet determination to follow the Lord, and I really appreciate that. We are sisters in the Lord. But I am offering myself to you beyond that. I would be delighted to own you as my sister, share joys and sorrows, to do things together."

"Thank you so much!" Edna returned. "You said that just at the right time. I need to leave the children somewhere tomorrow afternoon, and I'll be going past your place. I would drop them off about 1:30. Does it suit you?"

"It does," Helen said, smiling, "and I'll really look forward to that."

"You know, John," Edna said as the minivan hummed down the road on the way home, "I really enjoyed the service tonight. And I feel so blessed with the way our new family is reaching out to us. It feels so . . . so warm inside."

John smiled. "I'm glad you feel that way. Me too."

Edna held the tiny girl in her arms and smiled tenderly into the wee red face. So tiny—only two hours old! Gently she placed a kiss on the soft cheek and smiled up at John. His eyes met hers, savoring the moment.

"Which name shall we use, Mary or Bethany?" asked Edna.

"I think we should name her after your mother," said John.

"Mary, then. That's fine with me. Isn't she precious!"

"I asked my parents to tell yours," said John. "Father said he would drive over right away, so your parents will know very soon."

"Oh, John," exclaimed Edna, "I can't wait to show my mother her namesake! I wonder when she will come."

"I'm guessing it won't be long," John said with a smile.

Two hours later, Edna was just drifting off to sleep when a commotion awakened her.

"Grandma! Grandma! You haven't been here for a long time! We have a baby. Do you want to see her?" Edna heard Rachel chattering excitedly.

"Rachel!" exclaimed Mary. "How big you are getting! I came to see you and Mother and Paul and Hannah—and of course, the new baby. What is her name?"

"Mawe," chimed in Paul. "I like baby!"

"Where is Hannah?" Mary asked next.

"She's taking a nap," Rachel said. "Paul does too, sometimes. But I mostly don't anymore."

The bedroom door opened, and Doreen Kauffman entered quietly. "It's your mother, Edna," she said softly. "Shall she come in?"

"Anytime!" Edna exclaimed. "And, Doreen, could you bring us tea in about half an hour, please? I haven't seen my mother for several months."

"Oh!" Doreen exclaimed, sympathy in her voice. "I didn't know. I'll make the teatime really special. Shall I get out your china?"

"Please," said Edna.

Edna listened to her mother's soft footsteps as they entered the bedroom. She looked up into eyes that spoke volumes.

"Edna!" Mary exclaimed. "How are you?"

"Oh, Mother! I'm so glad you could come! Good, I'm doing good. I can hardly believe you're—here," she said with a catch in her voice.

Mary stooped to place a kiss on her daughter's cheek.
"This is little Mary Elizabeth," Edna said, holding the
tiny bundle toward her mother.

Mary reached out with eager hands and then caught
herself. "I almost forgot," she said. "Could you lay her on
the bed, please?"

A realization flashed over Edna. Her mother could not
take the baby from her arms.

"Sure," she said. "I understand. I just forgot too."

Eagerly Mary gathered the tiny form from the bed
and nestled into the rocking chair. "Oh, so little!" she
exclaimed. "I have never gotten over the wonder of a new-
born baby, Edna," she said in a choked voice. "With each
child, and each grandchild, it is still the same. What did
you say her name was?"

"Mary," Edna answered. "Mary Elizabeth. We named
her after you, Mother."

Little Mary began to squirm and cry. "There, there,"
Mary said soothingly as she patted and rocked the baby.
"So you are my little namesake. Thank you, Edna."

"You're welcome," Edna said, smiling at her mother.
"It was what John and I wanted to do."

Edna looked over at the doorway to see two small heads
peeking in.

"Come in, children," Edna invited. "The baby isn't
sleeping now. We will all want to visit with Grandma."

Rachel hurried to stand beside the rocking chair. Paul
advanced a little more hesitantly.

"Come to Grandma," Mary said softly, holding out her
hand to Paul. "You are growing to be such a big boy. Shall

I hold you?" Paul allowed himself to be lifted up beside the baby.

"He almost forgets me, Edna," Mary said, with a pang in her voice.

"I'm sure it will come back fast," Edna said. "Paul, remember how you drew another picture for Grandma last week?"

"It was such a nice picture," said Grandma. "I liked your tree."

So this was the Grandma who wrote him little notes and for whom he drew pictures. Paul smiled into Mary's face and relaxed against her shoulder.

The time passed quickly as Edna and Mary caught up with each other.

"I wrote to you about the Sunday we were taken into church," Edna said. "But I wished you and Father could have been there to share that with us."

"Yes," Mary replied. "I did too, because I care about everything that happens to you. But of course that would not have worked. Do you have friends?"

"Yes," Edna answered. "I really miss my old friends, but we are making new ones. Not only at Meadow Brook, but also at Pine Ridge. Sometimes we go to their Sunday evening services too. Ruth Miller and Helen Steiner are friends that I can relate to like sisters. Really, I guess I'm friends with all the sisters at church. I have a really good friend from Pine Ridge too. She is a young widow named Denise Horst."

"I know her," Mary said. "She just started getting milk from us. Denise is sweet."

"She is helping me with my new dress pattern," Edna said. "I wonder how you will like my new pattern and covering? I'm dressing modestly and simply, Mother. And that's the way I mean to stay."

"Good!" said Mary. "I knew you would, Edna. And yet I was so eager to see that you were staying faithful to godly principles. So many people drift away into living like the world, while they say they're living in grace. I want all of my children to be faithful to God."

"I know, Mother," Edna said softly. "I have been wanting to thank you for making sure that I knew how to become a Christian. It didn't really sink in at the time, but it added to the knowledge I had when John and I got serious about the Lord. Thank you for being a godly mother," Edna finished softly.

Tears filled Mary's eyes. "It is only my duty, Edna. I love you."

Doreen came in with a tea tray and set it on the dresser. With a smile toward Edna, she quickly left the room.

"Rachel," said Edna, "please go out to the barn and tell Daddy that Grandma is here."

John had barely entered the room when *his* parents arrived. He carried a still-sleepy Hannah in his arms.

"Well," said John, Sr., as he came through the doorway, "it looks like we're having a family gathering. How are Edna and the baby?"

"We're doing fine," Edna said happily. She smiled as her mother-in-law came over to peep into the tiny sleeping face. "Would you like to hold Mary Elizabeth?"

"I surely would," Grace said, smiling. "So she is your

mother's namesake. That's special," she said, turning to Mary.

Soon Mary had coaxed Hannah into her empty arms.

Two hours later, after everyone had left, Edna rested quietly, savoring each moment of her mother's visit.

Soon Doreen came in. "How was your visit?" she asked quietly.

"Wonderful!" breathed Edna. "I can't quite believe my mother was really here. I will store this away to cherish for a *long* time."

"I'm sure it was special," Doreen said. "I could tell she really loves you."

"Yes," Edna said, a tear slipping from the corner of her eye. "I know she does."

Mary drove the horse and buggy homeward with a soft smile on her face. The visit had helped to still the ache in her heart a little. Yet it also increased the longing to be able to freely spend time with Edna and her family. Sam would want to know about the baby. Could she remember everything?

Chapter 11

John pulled into the parking lot at Meadow Brook and turned off the minivan. Walking in, he joined the group at the back of the church.

"Well," Harold Steiner said, his sweeping glance taking in the whole group, "I believe we're all here. I'll give out the routes, and then we'll have prayer before we split up."

John listened as Harold divided the group into eight routes. Finally he turned to John. "John," he said, "since you don't have a route yet, you can help me." He placed a box of tracts into John's hands.

"Dear Lord," Harold prayed as the group bowed their heads, "please be with us as we pass out literature this afternoon. Lead us to the contacts You have for us. Open the hearts of the ones who will read these tracts. Help us to be godly, living examples of You as we spread the good news of salvation. In Jesus' Name. Amen."

John settled into the front seat of Harold's van. Turning

around, he nodded to Harold's children. "Hello," he said, looking at the oldest boy. "I know I've heard your names before, but I have trouble making everyone's name stick. You're Caleb?" he asked.

"I am," Caleb returned politely, "and this is Ernest, and this is Phebe."

"What are your ages?" John asked.

Ernest spoke. "Caleb is fourteen, I'm twelve, and Phebe is nine,"

Phebe's smile reminded John of Rachel's.

"I guess your family has done this route for a long time?" John asked.

"As long as I can remember," Caleb said.

"Yes," Harold added as he hopped energetically into the driver's seat, "we're going to the development just down the road here. Helen and I started doing this when we were first married. The community knows our children now. These are the three oldest. Then we have three more— younger ones." He glanced back at the children. "We cover a lot of territory fast now when we do the route."

Harold dropped the children off at Pine Street and parked the van near the entrance to Oak Street. "Here's where we get out," he said to John. "Stick these tracts in your suitcoat pockets. I already have some in mine. That way we won't run out before we cover the street. You take the houses on the left side of the street, and I'll take the ones on the right. If no one is around, just leave the tracts at the door."

John walked up to his first house. Rolling up two tracts, he caught them under the screen door handle. A lady was outside at the second house. Near the end of the street, a burly man came around the corner just as John was leaving the tracts at his door.

"What are you doing here?" he bellowed. "Didn't you see the No Soliciting sign at the mailbox?"

"I'm sorry, sir," John answered. "I'm new to this area, and I didn't notice. But I'll remove the tracts."

Taken aback by the quiet, unperturbed answer, the man stepped back, put his hand up to his chin, and surveyed John quietly.

"Well," he said, "I'm new too. I just moved in last week. Who . . . who are you?"

"I'm John Troyer. I go to the Mennonite church about two miles down the road here." John pointed to the left. "We're spreading the good news of salvation through Jesus Christ. Do you know Jesus Christ?"

"Know Him?" The man laughed dryly. "Mostly as a swear word, I guess. Never knew a Christian that was worth knowing. But you . . . you seem different."

"By the grace of God, I mean to be," John returned. "We're having services at the church tonight. Would you care to come?"

"Well, not tonight, I don't," the man replied. "I'm Tim Hutchinson. Come around again some Sunday, and we'll talk. I'm just newly divorced." He laughed hollowly. "Lost my wife and my children. So I'm just livin' it up now." He paused and finished softly, "But it's pretty hollow."

"Shall I come back tomorrow evening?" John asked.

"Ye-es," the man answered a bit uneasily. "Yeah, might as well. If you got anything to offer, I need it. Seven o'clock."

"All right. I'll be here. I'm glad to have met you, Mr.

Hutchinson," John said as he reached out to shake the man's hand in parting.

"I saw you had a contact over there," Harold said as the men walked back to the van. "Good or bad?"

"It started bad, but ended good," John replied. "The man and his wife divorced recently, and his life is all in pieces. He just moved in last week. His name is Tim Hutchinson. He invited me to come back to talk to him tomorrow evening."

"Well," Harold said, "we'll pray for you and Tim. I'm glad the Lord gave you words to say. It sounded a little tough to me."

John smiled as the truth struck him. It had been a bit tough. But the words he had needed had been there, without being planned.

"God just gives you words, John. That's His promise being fulfilled," Harold continued. "Remember how Jesus told his disciples they shouldn't worry about what they would say when they were brought before magistrates? Well, I believe in the same God when we pass out tracts."

John smiled at the short man beside him. Every word and every movement were packed with energy. Harold wasn't what you'd call polished, but his heart was in the right place.

Later, John told Edna about the contact.

"Just think, John," she said, "maybe Tim will become a Christian! I'll pray for you while you're gone."

The months were rolling by. Nine months had passed since John and Edna had first attended at Meadow Brook.

The fellowship had been strengthening and fulfilling in their lives.

John shaved, combed his hair, and looked in the mirror to check his appearance. Then he turned to Edna.

"Which child shall I help you get ready?"

"Please put Paul's shoes on," Edna requested. "All I have to do is finish packing the diaper bag."

With the last person in the vehicle, John pulled out into the driveway. Lady came over to the fence, neighing. John looked wistfully at the horse.

"Poor thing," John said. "Edna, Lady just doesn't get exercised enough. I hate to get rid of her, but there isn't time to ride her enough. If you're ready, I think I'll offer her to Father."

"I know we all like her," Edna said, "but it makes sense to sell her. And if she's at Father's, we could still see her."

"I want to go to Grandfather's on the way home!" Rachel exclaimed.

"We will if their lights are still on," John promised.

Edna turned to John. "I know they said this is a business meeting, but I don't know exactly what to expect."

"Brother Steve said we'll elect Sunday school super-intendents, trustees, and people for other offices like that. And then at the end, we'll talk about anything that affects church life, from putting a new roof on the church to out-reach ideas."

"It should be interesting," Edna answered. "I wonder if you'll be included in the elections?"

"We're pretty new," John answered. "I'm glad just to help the others—and learn how they do things. But I do really enjoy being involved with the brethren here."

"I'm so happy with the way you've been able to reach Tim Hutchinson," Edna said. "Remember the first time you went over to his place? He is much closer to God than he was then."

"Yes. We have to keep praying for that man. He knows what he needs to do. It's dangerous to be at that point if we aren't willing to go on in obedience to the Word."

Edna nodded.

At the church, Edna sat down beside Christina Miller's three little girls. Christina smiled from the other side.

The evening moved on rapidly. After devotions and reading the minutes of the previous year's meeting, the voting began.

After Harold Steiner was chosen as the Sunday school superintendent, Brother Edward spoke again. "We have two names on the slate for assistant Sunday school superintendent: Fred Zook and John Troyer."

Edna looked up sharply. What did the assistant superintendent do? Would John know how?

"Brother John has been chosen," Brother Edward announced. "Next we will be voting for two trustees."

The elections continued for several more minutes. Then open discussion began. It was decided to replace only the part of the roof that covered the entrance to the church instead of doing the whole building. Edna smiled as she listened to the brethren's differing opinions. A few possible changes were discussed about the way cottage meetings should be handled. Soon the service was over.

"Well, John," Edna said, "I feel more like I belong at

Meadow Brook all the time. How about you?"

"Yes," John answered. "I feel happy here too. So far, the way problems are handled here seems to be going the right direction. The Zimmerman boys are more reverent in church, and it seems like the family is fitting in with the group a little better. The older boys aren't allowed to sit in the balcony at the back during services anymore, like they had. I'd like to have a chance to get close to those boys."

"Do you feel comfortable about being assistant superintendent?"

"Fairly comfortable," answered John. "Harold and I enjoy working together. So I'll just follow his lead and ask questions. Harold's are so dedicated. People like that are the salt of the earth."

"By the grace of God, may we be the same kind of people," Edna said fervently. "It's not what other people think about us that matters. But what our lives say surely does."

"Exactly!" John affirmed.

"Daddy," Paul called from his seat, "I see Grandfather's house!"

"The lights are on!" cheered Rachel.

"All right," said John. "Then we'll turn in."

"Well, it's good to see you," John, Sr., said as he came to the door. He turned around. "Mother, John's are here!"

Grace emerged from the bedroom.

"Come in! Come in!" she said warmly. "We'll have cookies and hot cocoa. So just sit around the table."

"Grandmother," Rachel said with shining eyes, "I hoped

your lights would still be on when we came home. And they were!"

Grace squeezed Rachel and set Paul on his chair. Then she bustled over to heat the milk for cocoa.

"Father," said John, "I'm going to have to sell Lady. I just don't have time to take care of her properly. Do you want her?"

"Mother always did like Lady," John, Sr., said with a smile at his wife, "and our driving horse is getting quite old. Yes, we probably do. How much do you want for her?"

By the time the family left, plans had been made for Lady to be delivered the next day.

"We're saying good-bye to one of our last links with the Shady Glen era, Edna," John said quietly. "It hurts a little to let Lady go. But I know we are doing the right thing, and that's what matters. I don't have time—or money—to keep a horse. This little buggy here eats a lot of gas!"

Edna laughed softly with John. Then she answered, "I would feel worse about selling Lady if we wouldn't know who would be caring for her. But if we need to sell her, this is as good as it can be."

Edna listened attentively as John led in Sunday school devotions. John had been assistant superintendent now for four months. He and Harold took turns with devotions. "Lord," she prayed, "give John words that come from You."

Mary cried. Entering the nursery to feed her, Edna looked across the room to see Ruth with her two-week-old baby. Judith's wail filled the air. Finally, both babies were settled so that Edna could hear John's voice coming over the loudspeaker.

"Faithfulness is what counts," John was saying. "Just as the widow gave her two mites to God, we can give the little that we have to God. Then He can take that and make it into much more. God asks only for empty vessels that He can fill."

A tear moistened Edna's eye. "Lord," she prayed, "here are our vessels. Fill them with Yourself."

CHAPTER 12

Edna looked out the window at the drab, gray face of February. How cozy the warmth of the wood stove felt! She looked up from the dress she was hemming for Helen Steiner and smiled.

"With four growing girls and yourself, it must take a lot of sewing to keep everybody in dresses," Edna said. "I hope we can finish these two dresses for you before I go home this afternoon. I was so glad you invited me to come spend the day with you."

"It does take a lot of sewing," laughed Helen. "But don't forget you have three girls and yourself to sew for. So I won't be happy unless we also sew for you this afternoon."

"I know you said that," Edna replied. "So I have two cut-out dresses along. It's nice to visit and still get some of our work done."

"That is—as long as the children are happy," Helen said as she glanced across the room to the seven preschoolers playing, some on the floor and some at the kitchen table. The morning passed pleasantly.

"Who was the family that was visiting church on Sunday?" asked Edna, putting Mary into the highchair for lunch.

"They were Trevor and Linda Heisey," Helen answered. "Haven't you met them before? They've been coming almost every year to visit the Zimmermans. They've been friends with each other for a long time."

"How many children do they have?"

"I believe six or seven," Helen answered. "Harold said the oldest one is eighteen and the youngest one just started school. Did you hear that they're thinking of moving here?"

"No," said Edna. "Really?"

"Yes, they've almost closed on a property. He does computer programing in his own office, so he can take his work wherever he goes."

"I wanted to meet Linda," said Edna. "But then Mary was fussy, and I went out to sit in the van with her after church. What kind of people are the Heiseys?"

"Well, I'm not sure," Helen replied. "I guess you noticed the family is fairly liberal?"

"I did," Edna replied. "I also noticed that the children were whispering with their friends in church. John mentioned to me that they seemed to stick closely with the—would you say unconcerned—members from our congregation and didn't circulate much farther than that."

"A lot of our families are concerned about their coming," Helen said quietly. "It's something to pray about. We all add influence of some kind wherever we go."

Edna drove home thoughtfully. She would reach out to welcome another family in the same way they had been received. But what would the new family contribute to the congregation? She let out a sigh. If there were problems, surely the ministry would notice and take care of them.

"Well, Edna," John said at the supper table a few weeks later, "did you hear that we're helping the Heiseys move in this Saturday?"

"No. But I'll be glad to help. If the children are still sick, I'll send food and a note along with you."

"Brother Edward also said that Trent Martin has decided to attend regularly with us," added John.

"Who's that?" Edna raised her eyebrows.

"He's that blond-haired boy who has been coming a good bit lately. I hadn't realized that he wants to stay here. He used to go to Pine Ridge and lives at his uncle's place somewhere in the community."

"Oh," Edna said, remembering. "I think I know who you mean. Is he the one who sits with Vernon Zimmerman and Howard Hoover—the one with the really long hair?"

John nodded. He stood quietly with a thoughtful look on his face. He began to twirl the rooster tail at the back of his head.

"What are you thinking?" Edna asked finally.

"I'm not sure what to think," John answered. "I sensed that Brother Moses and Brother Steve are fairly concerned about the situation that's developing at church. But surely Trent and the Heiseys know what we stand for here. They'll have to prove themselves to become members."

Edna stood at the window, watching the moving truck back up to the empty house. The redbud trees were bursting into bloom. Glancing around the room, her eyes took in the sweeping lines of the cathedral ceiling. What a beautiful house this was!

The door opened, and Trevor and Linda stepped inside. "Oh, no!" Linda exclaimed sharply. "They weren't supposed to put the carpeting this far into the dining room. It was supposed to stop back beside the doorway. I'm sure I told you *twice* to tell them that, Trevor," she said, turning toward her husband.

"I did, Linda," Trevor replied. "But we'll take care of it. If you don't like it, I'll have them come out and change it."

Edna coughed. Linda looked toward the direction of the cough with a startled look on her face. A smile was quickly pasted on her reddening face. "I'm sure it will be fine," she said to her husband. "I didn't know you were here," she said, turning to Edna. "Now let me see. What is your name?"

"I'm Edna Troyer. My mother-in-law kept our little ones today so I could come. I know there's always so much to do on moving day, and we wanted to be here to welcome you."

Edna watched as Trevor quickly escaped out the door and helped John open the doors of the moving truck. For a moment she wanted to run too. Perhaps she should politely excuse herself for Linda's sake.

"It was so nice of you to come today," Linda said as she fumbled with her purse. "How many children do you have?"

"We have four living children," Edna replied, "and one in heaven. Our oldest child is almost six years old."

"So you will have a schoolchild next year," Linda said, looking up. "Are you ready for that?"

"I'm not sure," Edna laughed. "Let me know when there's something I can do."

"I will, after I know what's happening myself," Linda answered. "Oh! Here comes Nettie. She's a good organizer. We'll soon have things to rights here."

Gradually things began to take shape. Edna and Judith Kauffman emptied boxes of dishes and washed them. The kitchen cupboards began to look useful. Edna was almost glad when John came to see if she was ready to go home.

"Come over to our place sometime, Linda," she said as they parted. "We live only about two miles down the road. We'd be glad to have you stop in anytime."

"We'll do that! I'll be busy around here for a few weeks, but one of these days I'll find you," Linda promised.

"How was your morning?" John asked as they left the Heisey residence.

"I'm not quite sure, John," said Edna. "I tried to be careful so I wouldn't break anything. Linda's things are so beautiful. But I do know that the Heiseys will need friends, and I'm going to keep on being available if Linda wants me."

"Did something happen in the house after Trevor's got there?" asked John, a puzzled look on his face.

"Yes," said Edna. "Linda didn't see me at first, and she was blaming Trevor because the flooring hadn't been done right. But after she saw me, she told him it would be fine."

"Then that explains what he said to me when we were opening the truck," John said. "Trevor said something about moving being hard on women, and he hoped we would understand."

Edna looked up as Brother Edward began his announcement. "We're glad everyone could gather here in the school for a fellowship dinner," he said. "We're happy to welcome the Trevor Heisey family, who arrived a week ago, and also Trent Martin, who has been with us a little longer. We welcome the contributions of both to our congregation. We hope you will all feel at home here." Brother Edward paused and smiled at the newcomers. "Brother Andrew, would you please lead us in prayer before we eat?" he asked.

John and Edna filled their family's trays and found places at the tables for families with young children. Moses and Sally settled their family on the other side of the table.

"Did you talk to Trent?" asked Edna, on the way home.

"I did," said John. "It suits him to come for supper on Thursday night. That's the evening you said would suit you best, isn't it?"

"Yes. We'll be glad to get acquainted with him."

On Thursday morning the phone rang. John answered. "I'm sorry, Trent. Could we make it some other time? All right then. We'll just see how things work out."

"It doesn't suit Trent to come tonight, Edna," said John. "He said his schedule was too full to set another time."

Edna raised her eyebrows questioningly at John.

"I know what you're thinking," John said, "because I have the same thoughts. Something seems funny. But we'll just be here for Trent. Sooner or later he will need friends too, just like the Heiseys." John paused. "I hope they will all want the right kind of friends. That's what troubles me."

The phone startled John from the book he was reading. "Hello," he said. "No, James. We aren't busy. Sure, we would be glad if you'd drop in this evening. A friend? Sure. Bring him along too."

"James is coming with a friend," he said, turning to Edna. "For some reason he didn't say who he's bringing."

"We'll soon find out!" Edna smiled, a twinkle in her eyes.

John studied her face. Then he laughed. "Do you really think he's bringing Denise?"

"I didn't say that, John," Edna said, laughing. "But Denise has been dropping a few hints, like asking me what James was like when he went to Shady Glen, how long we have been friends with him, and things like that. I just got the feeling she was making a decision, though I really don't know anything."

"And you didn't say so," said John. "We'll see who comes in the door."

Ten minutes later the doorbell rang. John hurried to open it.

"Well!" he exclaimed. "Come in, James—and Denise! Is this an announcement or something?"

"Rather," said James with a smile. "Denise has done me the honor of accepting my friendship. And we wanted you to be among the first to know. Denise and I both call you some of our best friends."

Edna laughed as she greeted Denise. "James is almost

like a brother to us. So this is really special that he is courting one of my best friends."

Denise nodded and smiled shyly.

"You know, Edna," Denise began later as she helped Edna pop popcorn, "when Milton died, I thought I would never want to accept another man. But it's been over two years now since then. My children need a father, and I would be so grateful to have a godly husband to care for me and to share life with again. Am I considering this too soon?"

Edna thought quietly for a moment. "No, I don't think you are. The Bible says you're free to marry, and you give me the impression that you are no longer grieving. You don't usually cry now when you talk about Milton. Are you happy, Denise?"

Denise smiled and nodded. "So happy I sometimes pinch myself to make sure this is real. I don't deserve a principled, solid man like James. But I just wanted to make sure I'm on track and that I have your blessing."

Edna nodded reassuringly. "You both do."

Chapter 13

Edna sang as she fluffed up the pillows on the guest bed. A new school year was almost upon them, and Sister Karen Mast, the middle-grade teacher, would be boarding with them. This room would be like the one the Shunammite woman had prepared for Elijah. Carefully Edna ruffled the freshly ironed curtains on the curtain rods.

"Mama," asked Paul, "when is Sister Karen coming?"

"On Saturday. That means you will have to sleep two more nights. Then the next day Sister Karen will come."

Paul beamed happily into Edna's face. "I'm glad," he said eagerly. "I like Sister Karen."

"She plays with you, doesn't she?" Edna returned.

Paul nodded and ran off to find Rachel and Hannah. Edna picked up Mary and hurried downstairs to start supper.

Two days later, Rachel and Paul were watching at the window when the thirty-two-year-old teacher arrived.

"She's here, Mama!" they shouted.

Edna hurried to the door and welcomed Sister Karen inside.

"Come in," Edna welcomed her warmly. "We've been looking forward to this day!"

"Hello, everyone!" Sister Karen returned. "Here are Rachel and Paul. But where are Hannah and Mary?"

"Taking naps," returned Edna. "Your room is the one at the end of the hall upstairs. John thought you might like to have a room that is a little farther away from our noise. We want you to make yourself at home, Sister Karen."

"I already know that I will," Sister Karen returned. "Thank you so much! I never take it for granted when a family shares their home with me."

"Daddy," asked Rachel, on the way home from church one Sunday morning, "why do Rosalie and Betsy prance when they walk into church?"

John frowned and turned questioning eyes to Edna. Edna nodded back.

After dinner when John and Edna were alone, Edna said, "Rachel asked that question because of the way Rosalie Zimmerman and Betsy Heisey walk with their skirts so tight that they can't take full steps. They wear long dresses. But when you have a long dress that isn't very wide, you have to watch or you'll trip yourself."

"It seems like I see those girls together most of the time," John mused.

"Yes," answered Edna. "I often see Doreen Kauffman and Annette and Twila Miller trying to include them. But Rosalie and Betsy mostly stay in their own group—along with Regina Byler, who is chumming with them now too."

John nodded. "I think I'm noticing that Rosalie and Regina are dressing more like Betsy than they used to. Am I right?"

"Yes," Edna returned. "Their dresses are getting fancier, their stockings lighter, their hair more fluffed up, and their shoes more stylish. And they wear such tight sweaters—the things girls do when they're trying to fill a hole inside." Edna paused and looked out the window. Then she continued. "When Doreen was cleaning for me last week, she was telling me how things are going with the young girls. The girls seem so light and empty, and they are absorbed with boys. Rosalie Zimmerman and Trent Martin are sneaking off to talk whenever they find a chance."

"You know," said John, "I notice the same kind of things in some of the boys—mostly from those same families. The boys have their own set after church too. Longer hair, open shirt collars, and clothes that are more casual are becoming more common. Their attitudes seem careless—almost daring. Don't the parents notice that the children are cliquing?"

"Well," replied Edna, "I wonder if it doesn't start with the parents. Those three families get together about twice a week—mostly to have fun."

That evening John stood near the doorway to the anteroom, waiting for Edna. A group of boys sauntered into the anteroom from the other doorway and stood along the wall behind him.

"I hit ninety in my car last night," Tom Heisey bragged. "That thing really zoomed!"

"No, you didn't," Brian Zimmerman said with a grin. "You're just lying. You always do. I can't believe a word you say."

"Am not!" Tom returned.

"Yes, you are!" Kent Zimmerman put in.

The boys laughed loudly.

"Hey," said Charles Byler, "we'd better be quiet, or Caleb Steiner will come back here and ask us if we know what the Bible says about lying. Caleb will be the next preacher around here."

"He'd be a good one!" Brian exclaimed, guffawing.

Edna appeared, and John, sick at heart, moved over to the coatracks to help bundle up the children.

As the weeks went by, Edna enjoyed learning to know the schoolchildren through the stories both Rachel and Sister Karen shared at the supper table.

"How did school go today?" John asked Sister Karen at the supper table one evening.

"Well," Sister Karen said, "a good description for today would be to say that it was challenging."

"Oh?" questioned John. "Edna and I would be glad to hear about it later this evening."

"I'll come down about eight-thirty," Sister Karen replied.

The children were all settled in their beds when Sister Karen entered the living room. John put down the newspaper he was reading and looked up.

"Sit down," Edna welcomed.

Sister Karen settled wearily into an easy chair.

"I'm having some problems with disrespect," she said. "It starts with the children from a few families. But it doesn't take long for children who would normally behave to catch on to the mood too."

"I guess you've been talking to the school board chairman?" John asked.

"Yes. Brother Mervin understands the problem and suggested that I share the problem with the parents who are involved," Sister Karen replied. "So I did. But the parents don't feel their children are having a problem. They say their children don't have bad attitudes toward me personally and only respond this way when their teachers are too suspicious and picky."

"Hm-m." John nodded. "That is a problem. Are the children trying to do things behind your back?"

"Yes," Sister Karen responded. "I need eyes in the back of my head this year. They pass notes when my back is turned and whisper at recess with withering glances in my direction. When I need to punish one of them, the others criticize me and decide if they think I was fair or not.

"Nettie tells me that I should be trusting the children to tell me what really happened when a misdemeanor takes place, and Trevor tells me that I should be having fun with them, to build a trusting friendship."

"I've never taught school," John said slowly, "but anyone who has worked with children very long knows that it doesn't work to put disrespectful children in charge of the situation."

"We had a similar problem in the upper-grade classroom at the school where I used to teach," Edna said. "But we couldn't move on to a happy, orderly classroom until the school board entered into the situation. They put things firmly in place and required respect for all the teachers. When that happened, the children began to respect issues of right and wrong too."

"I know what you mean," Sister Karen said. "A fear of God causes us to respect all the authority levels God places over us—or it works the other way around."

"And discipline is necessary to put that fear in place in children's hearts. They really should learn that at home," John added. "But if they haven't, then it must be put in place at school. Is Mervin helping you with the problem?"

"Mervin is doing his best to support me," Sister Karen explained. "Discipline is the sticky part. I have been using discipline, and the parents have been objecting. News travels by the grapevine about what supposedly happened at school, and it gets quite confused by the time it reaches the last person."

"Do the parents ask you what happened?" asked John.

"Rarely," Sister Karen replied. "Nettie said they've learned that they have to listen to what their children are telling them, and trust them—or the children won't talk to them. Sam Byler and Bill Horst have told me about the same thing. So the twisted stories that the children take home are the basis for the case the parents are building about the way they think school is being handled."

"What are the unhappy parents saying?" asked John.

"Well," said Sister Karen, "the charges vary. But basically they're saying that I'm too strict and critical and that I pick on their children." She paused. "Have you noticed the clique that several of the families have?"

John nodded. "We have. You mean the Zimmermans and the Heiseys?"

"Yes," said Sister Karen. "They're the main ones. Then Sam's and Bill's children—they are cousins, you know—also join in with them. And it becomes a large group of children facing me rebelliously at school. Without more help from the board, I cannot handle it. In the twelve years I have taught school, I have never taught in a school that allows things to operate quite like this."

"What is Brother Mervin doing now to work out the situation?" asked John.

"He's talking to the ministry," said Sister Karen, "and things aren't moving too fast from there. Brother Mervin says to move cautiously right now. I never give a punishment without talking to him first. I think he feels troubled about something, but he doesn't tell me what it is."

"Well," said John, "this is something to pray about. Shall we do that right now?"

Quietly the three knelt to cast the burden on the Lord.

"John," said Edna when they were alone again, "are nonsupportive parents being allowed to run the school? What's wrong?"

"I don't know, Edna," John replied. "But if what Sister Karen is telling us is correct, the problem is serious."

"Edna," said John, "James said they're having meetings at Pine Ridge this weekend. Shall we spend the day there on Sunday?"

"Sure," said Edna. "Maybe Sister Karen would like to go along."

"I don't have a program to show her," John said, "but she's certainly welcome."

Sunday afternoon found the Troyers and Sister Karen sitting with the group of worshipers at Pine Ridge. The moderator stood up to introduce the first speaker.

"Brother Clair Martin, from Silver Creek, Pennsylvania, will bring us the first message of the afternoon: 'The Biblical Framework of Discipline.' May we give him our attention."

Edna listened carefully as the aged man launched into his subject.

"Discipline was not meant to feel good," Brother Clair said. "I don't like discipline. Do you?" he asked, his clear gaze sweeping over the crowd. "Yet discipline is important, for it is the means by which God brings our carnal hearts to repentance.

"It is true that discipline does not change the heart. Rather, discipline brings the heart to a point where it must choose to repent and surrender to God or to continue in rebellion. And when we choose to repent and bow before God, our hearts are changed. We are cleansed from our carnality to honor and love Him.

"Repentance is the only way our hearts can be affected. We must have the fear of God firmly in place, because God sets the pace—not man. Authorities need to resolve problems in light of the principles in God's Word. We dare not let liberal, carnal factions control issues.

"The current worldly trend is to question authority and discipline and to look for an easier way—one that is not so hard on the flesh. Psychology tells us to make things appealing so that the individual will want to produce the desired effect. 'Give the rabbit a carrot to chase,' they say. It has become popular to sidestep the unpleasantness of discipline by focusing on positive things the person is doing, encouraging him, being understanding, or building him up.

"But the flesh dies only when it is starved, not when we step softly around it. What we feed grows, and what we starve dies.

"What is the alternative to not using discipline? When problem issues are being ignored to 'keep peace,' sin and stagnation set in like an infection. What is allowed becomes the norm, and entire bodies of people are affected.

"The suggestion that discipline is not effective is not a relevant thought. Standing for truth does not mean people will like us or that people with sin in their lives will respond. But truth forms the dividing line where God requires each person to make a choice for Him. It is the only way to change lives.

"Jesus told us that following truth will split relationships. Turn in your Bibles to Matthew 10:32–40. We will read that now.

" 'Whosoever therefore shall confess me before men, him will I confess also before my Father which is in heaven. But whosoever shall deny me before men, him will I also deny before my Father which is in heaven. Think not that I am come to send peace on earth: I came not to send peace, but a sword. For I am come to set a man at variance against his father, and the daughter against her mother, and the daughter in law against her mother in law. And a man's foes shall be they of his own household. He that loveth father or mother more than me is not worthy of me: and he that loveth son or daughter more than me is not worthy of me. And he that taketh not his cross, and followeth after me, is not worthy of me. He that findeth his life shall lose it: and he that loseth his life for my sake shall find it. He that receiveth you receiveth me, and he that receiveth me receiveth him that sent me.'

"Remember this," Brother Clair said in closing. "Jesus said that if we lose our selfish lives for Him, we will find real life. So discipline is a blessing because it aids us in dying to the bondage of selfishness and sin. When we respond to God, we walk into the glorious liberty God has for us. Then we are free to carry His torch of truth."

As Brother Clair sat down, the congregation sat quietly, deep in thought.

"Edna," said John as they sat on the couch at home, reviewing the day, "that was a message from God. It was thoroughly Biblical and strengthens me in knowing what is right."

"You're right," said Edna. "I haven't heard any messages like that for a while. When we left Shady Glen and came to Meadow Brook, I was so eager for the encouraging, positive, nurturing messages we were hearing. But my heart is hungry to hear more messages full of conviction like this one. Because we really need them."

"Exactly," said John. "We don't produce godliness by patting people on the back."

Edna nodded quietly, and they both sat in silence, deep in thought.

CHAPTER 14

Brother Edward remained at the pulpit after the normal announcements had been made. "There is one more announcement to make this morning. Brother Trevor and Sister Linda and their family and Brother Trent have been with us for about eight months now. We are preparing to take them in as members sometime before the next Communion date. We are grateful for their contribution and pray that God will make us all a blessing to each other. If anyone has something to say about this issue, contact one of the ministry in the next several weeks."

"Edna," John said after lunch that day, "I won't be eating supper. I want to fast and pray about the new members about to be taken in."

Edna shook her head. "Doesn't Brother Edward know what their lives say?" she asked.

"It's a concern to me too," said John. "Several of us plan to meet with Brother Edward tomorrow evening to share our concerns about the ones coming in and the way they're affecting the congregation."

"I'll try to keep the children quiet, John. And if I have a chance, I'll slip in to pray with you too."

"I understand you've come to share your concerns about the new members about to be taken in," said Brother Edward as he seated John Troyer, Mervin Miller, and Joshua Miller. "Feel free to share. We want to hear. That's why we made the announcement."

Brother Edward listened as each brother aired his concerns. Then he nodded.

"I realize the incoming members have issues in their lives that they need to deal with," Brother Edward said. "As you say, their attitude toward life is carefree instead of being committed, and several of them are not yet conformed to our discipline. But they have made a few changes, and I am looking for the rest to come. I have that confidence.

"You say that some of our own members are being influenced by them in a negative way. But I am also sorry for the poor influence our people have had on Trevor's family and on Trent.

"I would caution you brethren on a few points. I'm glad you are all men of conviction. That is good. We need you all. But don't let your convictions become a point of harshness or criticism in meeting the needs of others."

For a moment, John, Mervin, and Joshua sat quietly, stunned.

Finally, Brother Mervin cleared his throat. "Brother Edward," he began, "you say that you are sorry for the poor influence our congregation has had on Trevor's and Trent. Doesn't that mean that there are two sets of problems to be taken care of—the problems in our own membership, as well as the problems in people who want to become members?"

Brother Edward nodded. "I see what you mean."

"Another question," began John. "You mentioned that we should be tolerant of other people. I would understand that—if we were talking about whether we think Fords or Chevys are better. And there are areas of application where we come out a little differently. Those would be personal differences. But aren't we looking at matters of right and wrong when we look at carnality and infringements on our standard of discipline?"

"I'm hearing what you're saying," Brother Edward answered.

"What is our discipline really intended to be?" asked Joshua.

"Well," answered Brother Edward, "it is a guide to help us make applications to the Bible. But I understand the thought you are sharing—that a standard of discipline should be followed, or we will lose ground and apostatize. Given time, I think we will see Trevor's and Trent growing to fit in here. I see real potential for Christian growth and development as we nurture and encourage them."

John was quiet as he and Edna closed their day.

"How did it go, John?" Edna asked gently.

John related the dialogue he, Mervin, and Joshua had shared with Brother Edward. Then he frowned and shook his head.

"I'm baffled, Edna. We could not really get anywhere with Brother Edward. Am I completely wrong, or are there concepts about church life Brother Edward just doesn't see?"

"The Bible will always stand, John," said Edna. "I hear some of the sisters talking about the 'Christian' books they are reading about relationships, about being hard on yourself and lenient toward others, and that sort of thing. Do you think that's good?"

"No," John answered. "We all just need to do what's right and expect everybody else to do the same thing. That's what the Bible teaches. We can never excuse sin for the sake of relationships. When we're preoccupied with the 'currently correct' thought about being nonjudgmental, accepting others, and using encouragement instead of discipline to bring out the best in people—maybe we have been reading too many books other than the Bible."

"I was thinking the same thoughts," answered Edna.

John's face relaxed. Then he continued. "God's Word calls for repentance—not gradual social change because we have been made to feel good about ourselves. We don't need to become intimidated, Edna. If we stick with the Word, we will always be on solid ground. And by the grace of God, we'll do that."

Several weeks later, Trevor and Linda Heisey, their teenage children, and Trent Martin were taken in as members. Many of the church members went home with heavy hearts.

John quickly counted out the tracts for literature distribution. Would he be ready in time? None of the other committee members were there to help him that day.

Gradually the group assembled. John looked up in surprise as Tom Heisey sauntered up to join the group at the back of the church, dressed in blue jeans and a bright, striped jacket. John scanned the group. How should he respond? None of the ministry was here to confer with, and there were only several minutes left until starting time. Would another trend be starting if he let this slip?

John thought quietly and then walked over to Tom.

"Tom," he said, "could you help me bring more tracts from the storage room?"

"Sure," Tom said. He followed John to the basement.

"Please put these on the front seat of my vehicle," John said. "The main reason I asked you to help me was so I could talk to you in private, Tom. I noticed your jacket and blue jeans. Do you consider these your dress clothes?"

"Well, no," Tom mumbled, looking down.

"We ask people to come in their dress clothes to pass out literature," John said. "Casual clothing gives people the image that our Christianity is also casual. We want people to know that the Gospel we offer is real and changes lives. I also like to wear my suitcoat because I'm glad to be associated with a group of people who are known to be set apart from the world.

"We appreciate that you came to help. Why don't you go home and change, and then you can meet me on my route to help me?"

"No, thanks," Tom said. "I'll just skip it this afternoon, and the next time I'll know what to wear."

The phone rang. John jumped up from the supper table.

"Will you be at home this evening?" Brother Edward asked. "Betty and I would like to come over."

"Sure, that will be fine! We'll look forward to that."

"I'll enjoy a visit with Betty," Edna said, smiling. "We haven't really chatted at length for several weeks."

"Brother John," Brother Edward said after small talk had evaporated, "I got a call from Trevor this afternoon. He said that you sent Tom home from literature distribution because he wasn't dressed right. I just wanted to ask you what happened."

"That's partly right and partly wrong," John said. "He came in a flashy jacket and blue jeans when it was about time to start. No one from the committee or the ministry was there to confer with. So I did the best thing I knew to do. I hope I did the right thing.

"I asked Tom to carry tracts for me and took him to the supply room, where I could talk to him in private. I told him we don't want people to wear casual clothes when we pass out literature, because it gives the impression that the Gospel we offer is also casual. Then I suggested that he go home, change his clothes, and come back to join me on my route.

"Tom was respectful. He said he wouldn't come back this time, but that he would know what was expected the next time."

"Did you encourage him, John?"

John scratched his head. "Well, if I remember right, I told him we were glad he came to help," John replied. "Is that encouragement?"

"Probably," Brother Edward replied. "The point is this. By making an issue of his clothes, Tom feels rejected, and now the Heiseys are upset. Wouldn't it have been better to have been positive and been glad that he wanted to help spread the Gospel?"

Something knotted in the pit of John's stomach. "Brother Edward, how do you feel about trends of carnality in church life?" John asked.

"Well," said Brother Edward, "they aren't good. I'm concerned as much as some of you brethren are, that within the last year, wearing plain suits, using the greeting, and living and dressing like a Christian are being challenged. It brings me deep pain to see some of our young people following carnal patterns, while their parents defend them." Brother Edward shook his head and continued.

"But the way to reach our carnal members must be in ways they can accept, or we won't be effective. People will leave our church if we push them too fast. God is a God of grace and mercy. I want to reach their hearts for God. That's where change is meaningful."

John sat quietly for a moment, with his brow furrowed. "This is a subject that has been troubling me quite a bit lately. Do you mind if I ask you some more questions, Brother Edward?"

"That's fine," Brother Edward responded.

"I mean to be respectful to you when I ask this," John began. "Do we change people's hearts by allowing them to lie, live with a partying spirit, break the law, and disregard the principles in our rules and discipline—and still remain a part of the church?"

"No," Brother Edward replied. "No. I'm just hoping, by giving them time, that God will work in their hearts and bring them to Himself."

"How are carnal people brought to repentance?" John asked. "Isn't it by law? Sin is direct opposition to God. There is no nice way to confront sin. When we come to God, we have to do a complete turnaround and forsake sin. That happens when law confronts us, and we choose either to die to self and live to God or to continue in our sins.

"My children would hit and scream if we wouldn't punish them for such things. But when we draw lines for them, and it becomes more unpleasant to be punished than to do what they want to do, they learn to obey. And they are so much happier afterward, and so is our home."

"I know what you mean," Brother Edward said. "Discipline isn't easy or pleasant. It hurts. And yet it really must be done in church life."

John nodded and continued. "Now let's look at the schoolchildren who are making problems in school and at the carnal young people our congregation is dealing with. Apparently their parents are not putting law into their children's lives by requiring them to be accountable for their actions or punishing them for infractions. Instead, the parents defend them."

"Yes." Brother Edward shook his head sadly. "I know that all too well. When I approach the parents about an issue, they tell me other people are doing the same thing and getting by with it. Or they say that I am driving their children away."

"So then, what is the way to a pure church?" John

asked. "By allowing liberalism in our congregation, do you see carnal people becoming spiritual—or do you see more people joining the carnal trend?" John asked.

Brother Edward sat with bowed head. "Brother John," he said, "you're right. We're going the wrong way."

"Brother Edward," John asked, "may I ask one more question? I am reading 1 Timothy right now. Chapter 5, verse 20 says, 'Them that sin rebuke before all, that others also may fear.'

"Is it a good objective to let the church go down, while tolerating carnality among the members and hoping that they will change if they are given more time? Or is it right to maintain a holy church that has something to offer, because people are forced to decide if they want to be a part of the church or a part of the world?"

Brother Edward wept. "John," he said, "you are right. Obviously God wants a pure church. I just don't know how to reach the carnal ones."

John sat quietly and swallowed. What more could he say than he had already said?

"Brother Edward," he finally said quietly, "does the verse we just talked about answer that question?"

"Yes, John," Brother Edward replied heavily. "It does."

CHAPTER 15

Edna stood at her kitchen window. The garden was doing nicely, with the first planting of green beans just ready to pick. Flitting from the pasture fence, two bluebirds flew to the birdhouse John had made for her. Edna smiled contentedly. Would this pair be nesting?

Edna's eyes sparkled as she noticed Moses' minivan coming in the lane. She hurried to change her apron.

"Come in!" Pleasure lilted in Edna's voice as she welcomed Sally. "I've been at home so long since Conrad has been born and the children have been sick, that I'm so glad to see—" Seeing only dull grief in Sally's eyes, Edna's words froze in midair. She paused and leaned forward. "Sally! What's wrong? Is it one of your children?"

Sally only walked over to the table, laid her head on her arms, and sobbed. Placing tiny Conrad in the bassinet, Edna moved toward the table. She waited quietly beside Sally.

At last Sally raised her head and began to talk. "Oh, it's been awful, Edna! We've had all this conflict and apostasy in our congregation in the last year and a half. And now I just left the hospital—Moses is still there—knowing that Tom Heisey will be . . ." Sally put her head down and cried again.

"Is he still living, Sally?" Edna prodded.

"Yes, he is," Sally began again, "and he is expected to live. But he is paralyzed from the waist down."

"Oh, no!" exclaimed Edna. "So young!"

"And the way it happened is so sad. Tom Heisey and Vernon and Brian Zimmerman were out running around late last night. The police say Tom was going eighty-five around a curve when he hit the tree."

"Are the other boys hurt?" asked Edna.

"Vernon has a huge cut on his face where he hit the windshield, and Brian has a broken leg. He was in the back seat.

"Now Andrew and Nettie are blaming Trevor and Linda for letting it happen, and Trevor and Linda are so upset they're hardly talking to anybody. And our ministry is trying to help and comfort the boys. The boys all feel terrible, though it seems they are more concerned about being caught than about their sin.

"And Tom . . . will never walk again. What if he had been our boy, Edna?"

John and Edna moved quietly through the hospital halls. "I hope Conrad will be all right for your mother while we're here," Edna said.

"We won't stay long," John promised. "We'll go see the Zimmerman boys first. They're both in the same room."

John walked quietly into the hospital room. Brian lay on his back with his leg in traction. He moaned softly. Vernon's face was so swathed in bandages that it would have been difficult to recognize him on sight.

John stopped between the beds.

"Hello, boys," he said evenly. "How are you doing today?"

Both boys turned toward John and Edna. "Terrible," muttered Brian.

"I guess about as good as we could hope to, under the circumstances," answered Vernon.

"We were sorry to hear about your accident," John said.

"Tom got the worst end of the deal," Vernon said. "If only . . ." Then he covered his face with his hands to hide the tears that were dripping onto his bandages.

"The Lord cares about all of us," John said softly. "We're very sorry this happened. But if you seek the Lord through this, good can come from something that would otherwise have been only a tragedy. We'll all be praying for you and Tom."

"Thank you, John. I appreciate that," answered Vernon. "Mother and Father were just here, but they went down to the cafeteria to get some food. Thanks for coming," Vernon finished.

"What will I say to Linda, John?" asked Edna as she and John walked to the intensive care unit.

"Just depend on God to give you words," John said. "God is the one who knows where each of us are in our personal experience and how we are feeling in our grief. Sometimes just being there is the most important thing. Holding someone's hand and saying 'I'm sorry' is sometimes the loveliest thing we can do for each other."

John and Edna found Trevor and Linda in the ICU waiting room.

"I'm so sorry, Linda," Edna said as she approached Linda.

There were no words. Linda simply cried as Edna sat beside her and held her hand.

Trevor had little to say. "Thank you for coming," he said wretchedly. "We can't go in for another hour. They're doing a procedure on Tom, so we're just passing the time here."

"Is there anything we can do?" asked John.

"I think everything is taken care of," answered Trevor, "but we appreciate the offer. Just pray for miracles."

"We will," promised John. "We have a God of miracles. Sometimes the greatest miracle is the good that God brings from our sorrow."

John and Edna's footsteps echoed hollowly as they walked to the hospital exit. Edna's heart cried.

Though the congregation reached out to share with the Heiseys, they remained aloof. After the accident, none of the family ever returned to Meadow Brook. When Tom was stabilized enough to move, the family went back to Kentucky to be near family and a reputable rehab center. And though the congregation continued to pray for them, there was only minimal reciprocation.

After the initial shock of the boys' accident wore off,

life began to return to normal in the Meadow Brook congregation. After he was released from the hospital, Vernon Zimmerman came to Meadow Brook for a few weeks. Then he began attending at Living Waters, with plans to move his membership. When Brian's leg was out of traction, he came to church with his family, using crutches.

For a few weeks, the spiritual temperature among the young people improved slightly, with a few commitments. However, the carnal seeds that had been allowed to spread during the last year and a half continued to grow and bear fruit, and the new commitments soon paled.

Brother Edward stood up in the pulpit with a deep sense of burden etched on his face. "This morning," he said, "I am going to preach about our purpose and goal in life. Are we carnal, or are we spiritually-minded?

"I have been noticing some burdens that our congregation is bearing. When we live according to our flesh, we produce the fruit of the flesh. When we live according to the Spirit, we produce the fruit of the Spirit.

"What are each of you choosing? To follow God, or to follow the devil? Are you moving closer to the world in your interests, or closer to heaven and following God?

"Young people, I have some things to say to you. What are you talking about? What consumes your thoughts? And what about the way you drive and dress? What kind of songs do you sing? What kind of tapes do you have under your seats? These are the fruits of your lives. Are your choices taking you toward God, or away from Him?"

"Lord," prayed John, "help me to live according to Your Word. Thank You for the blood of Jesus that cleanses us from sin and consecrates us to serve You!"

"I really appreciated your burden, Brother Edward," John said after the service. "Unless our lives are affected by the Gospel, our hearts are not the property of Jesus Christ."

Mervin Miller chimed in. "And unless we use discipline in our families and in our churches, the cause will be lost in our young people."

Brother Edward surveyed Mervin thoughtfully and then nodded his head.

"We have an issue to take care of before we go home tonight," Brother Edward said on Wednesday evening. "It is time to replace another school board member. Brother Bill Horst has fulfilled his term, leaving Brother Mervin Miller and Brother George Shank on the board. We will be voting between Brother Joshua Miller and Brother John Troyer."

"I'm surprised I was elected," John shared with Edna on the way home. "People know we are conservative."

"But then the largest percentage of our families do care, John," Edna said. "If Brother Edward would take a different position, we could still have a nice congregation. I think a lot of people are seeing what is happening and are ready for something different."

At the first school board meeting John attended, Brother Mervin focused on the disrespect issue.

"I think it's time to simply step in and set the pace at school," Mervin said fervently. "We've been moving gently long enough. We need to discipline the spirit of rebellion."

Brother Edward leaned back in his chair. "What

kind of discipline would you use?" he asked. "Writing assignments?"

"No," Brother Moses spoke up. "We've tried that, and it hasn't worked much better than a mild slap across the hands. The discipline policy of our school states that a spanking or expulsion is necessary to punish continuing disrespect."

"I agree with Brother Mervin and Brother Moses," Brother Steve said. "We need to bring punishment at the point where we want to see improvement. I make a motion that we begin using either a spanking or expulsion for students who keep on challenging the teachers."

"I second the motion," said John.

"Now wait, brethren," Brother Edward said, rising from his chair. "I agree that we need to do more, but don't be so hasty! We must think of relationships. At the same time we try to make things happen, we *must* build relationships."

After a long discussion, the meeting ended without any motions being accepted.

"I don't know, Edna," John said, when he came home. "We can't do much if Brother Edward doesn't let us. I didn't realize the situation was this bad. Now I understand why Mervin couldn't do more to help Sister Karen with the problems she was facing last year."

"I can't blame her for not coming back again," Edna sighed, "but we miss her." Edna paused and smiled at John. "We can still pray, John."

Edna looked over the audience that had gathered at Pine Ridge. Today was James and Denise's wedding day. Edna smoothed her skirt and looked up at John. He smiled reassuringly. At John's nod, she stepped into the aisle beside him and walked toward the waiting front bench. Presently James and Denise seated themselves between her and John. How special to share this day with them!

Edna stood quietly beside Denise as Brother Brendon Weaver, the bishop, moved into the marriage ceremony. The simple beauty of the service had filled her heart with peace. Could it be that it had been only eight years since she and John had stood before Bishop Sam in the living room at home and made their vows? So much had happened since then. How she loved John!

"I now pronounce you husband and wife," Brother Brendon intoned. Tears filled Edna's eyes.

Many hands were thrust into Edna's as the crowd moved through the receiving line. Edna smiled into each face. But in her mind, she could not forget the look of tender joy in Denise's moist eyes or the strong resolve and happiness in James's.

"Well," said John as they left the reception hall, "I am so happy for James that it almost hurts inside."

"I know," Edna said quietly. "I marvel at how God works. Did you see how happy Denise was? And the children? They love James so much."

John nodded.

"The service and reception were so simple and beautiful, John. Everything was in order. It felt so good. Do you know what I mean?"

"I do, Edna. Sometime in the next year or two, we may need to make a decision about our future."

"I hope so much that things clear up, and our families at Meadow Brook can all be blessed," said Edna. "John, I love everybody so much! They took us in like family."

"I know," said John. "We owe them a lot."

CHAPTER 16

John breathed a sigh of relief. He was tired. Now his Sunday evening topic, "Godly Music," was over. Preparing for it had taken a lot of work, but the study had been a real blessing to him.

"I really appreciated your topic, Brother John," Melvin Kauffman said, shaking his hand. "I think I'll go through my tapes when I get home." Several other brethren joined the discussion. John felt strengthened as the group shared.

Leaving the church, John carried the sleeping baby against his shoulder and held the door for Edna and the children.

"It surely is dark tonight!" exclaimed Edna as they went down the steps and walked away from the light. "But the air is fresher. Doesn't that feel good after a hot August day?"

"It does," agreed John. His eyes scanned the dark night sky. "I can find only two stars." Suddenly he stopped. "Where is Paul? I thought he was with you and the girls, Edna."

"We'll go in to look for him," offered Edna. "You have the baby."

John moved back into the sheltered corner beyond the porch light to relax against the wall. As his eyes adjusted, he began to see more stars.

The church door burst open. Soon John heard voices.

"Yeah!" It was Trent Martin's voice, with the high-pitched squeak he used when he was trying to look tough. "Preacher John really told us straight tonight, didn't he? Well, it's not gonna change me. I'm gonna listen to my country and rock CDs. It's no one else's business, and no one needs to know."

Three boys moved around the corner of the building and stood in a circle, blocking John's exit.

"Well," Brian Zimmerman said, "if Edward comes around to see Dad about my music—and he probably won't—Dad knows what to do. He'll just tell Edward that Mom won't stay if we get picked on, and Edward will back off real fast."

The boys laughed loudly. But the hollowness of the boys' facade struck John's heart with pity.

"Yes," Howard Horst chortled. "Old Ed certainly doesn't intend to be harsh or turn anybody away! We know how to handle him. If we're nice to him, he might even pat us on the back." John could see just well enough to catch a sly wink on Brian's face.

"Good evening, boys," John said steadily.

Howard and Trent whirled around. Brian was the first to regain his composure. "Uh, sorry!" he said. "We didn't mean to pen you in like that, John."

"That's quite all right, boys," John answered. "I'm just waiting for Edna to find Paul. I was sure you would let me out again."

The boys laughed shakily. Howard spoke. "You, uh, you won't tell anybody, John?"

"What are you referring to, Howard?" asked John.

"I mean, uh, the things we said here. We were just talking. We probably shouldn't have said them."

"What would you say was wrong with the things you said?" asked John.

The boys stared uncomfortably at the ground. Finally Howard spoke.

"Well, we know we're supposed to respect Brother Edward . . . and . . . uh, not have worldly things . . . like bad music."

There was silence.

"You know, boys," John began, "I used to be right where you are. I went for country music and then to rock music, trying to fill the empty place inside my spirit. I dabbled in drink and drugs, partly just to look tough to my friends. I didn't care what my parents and the church said. But I was so empty inside, and the hole just kept getting bigger as I got deeper into sin.

"But when I found God, all that changed. The sinful things that I used to crave sickened me. Coming to know God personally and living for Him has been the most blessed thing that has ever happened to me. No, not easy. But blessed, because I am at peace with God now."

"We'll think about that," Howard said softly. Then suddenly he blurted, "Sometimes—sometimes I wish you were my dad so someone would make me do what I know I should do."

As John searched the three faces looking at him, the expressions on Trent's and Brian's faces wilted.

"Boys," John said with feeling, "I'll be glad to talk to you anytime. Why don't you come over tomorrow evening, and we can sit down and talk. I can tell you what happened to me, and we can discuss the things you need to work through."

"I got things to do tomorrow evening," Brian responded, "but thank you."

"I'll see," Howard said.

Trent shuffled off, muttering, "See you boys later."

Just then the church door opened again, and Edna came around the corner with Rachel, Paul, Hannah, and Mary.

"Good night, boys," John said as he stepped out to meet his family. "I'll be praying for you."

A few months went by. John leaned forward as he listened to Mervin and Harold.

"Do you want more popcorn?" Edna asked, coming into the living room to serve the guests. "I'll just leave the bowl in here with you."

John smiled. "Thank you. We appreciate that." Taking the bowl, John turned his attention back to the conversation he was sharing with the group.

"So we all see the same problems that are being allowed in our congregation," John said quietly. "Materialistic lifestyles, poorly attended prayer meetings, worldly dress patterns, and carnality expressed in different ways. Do you think there will be a future here at Meadow Brook for our families? I don't think I want to raise my children here unless things change."

"I certainly hope there will be a future," Mervin said.

"There should be, if enough families with conviction stay," Harold said. "But I sometimes wonder myself. I don't know if we can stay unless Brother Edward is willing to take action when problems come up."

"It isn't that there is no discipline at all," John added. "But what gets addressed is usually only the top few more serious things, while the rest go on unresolved. And that means there is always tension. I am weary of continually bucking things. Is this the way God wants church life to be?"

"No," said Mervin, "it isn't. We all know that. But, John, perhaps God has brought you 'to the kingdom for such a time as this.' "

"Yes!" exclaimed Harold. "You can't know what an encouragement you have been to us, John."

"Well, you and your families have surely blessed us too," said John. "I don't know what the future holds. But like Joshua said, 'As for me and my house, we will serve the LORD.' "

"Amen!" Mervin and Harold breathed together.

"I haven't been noticing Trent at church the last few Sundays," John said, "and I'm wondering about him. Does anyone know anything?"

"Last week Brother Edward told me Trent isn't coming to church anymore," said Harold. "Melvin Kauffman has been telling his father about the things the boys are doing. When Brother Edward talked to Trent about his rock music, Trent didn't repent. Instead, he became angry and said he was not coming back anymore. And he hasn't. They say he moved to West Virginia, where he has an uncle." Harold shook his head sadly.

"That's too bad," said Melvin, with a troubled frown. "I wish I could help the boy. Trent has many leadership qualities, and he puts his whole being into what he does. We must fast and pray."

"Edna," said John, "I hate to ask you this question so soon again, but we need a place for Sister Orpha Wenger to board for the last half of the school year. Our old farmhouse has more room than most of the other families have, and some of the families with a room to share would have a student in Sister Orpha's classroom. Would you mind boarding a teacher again?"

"No," said Edna, "I don't mind, John. If I need help with the work, you always see to it that I have a maid. And maybe Sister Orpha will be the kind that will pitch in. A few things out of place won't matter if we can make Sister Orpha feel welcome."

John's smile spoke volumes, though he said little. "What a blessing you are, Edna!" he said tenderly as he left for work.

School board work continued to be hard work. John returned from late board meetings with a weary look on his face.

"It isn't that the problems would be so hard to take care of, Edna," he explained when he returned from the November meeting. "The issues are clear. But we are required to step carefully between so many people while we try to do what needs to be done, and that wears me out."

"What are you working on now?" asked Edna.

"Right now we're focusing on the upper-grade room. Brother Brian is having trouble with a careless attitude toward grades, and there is a lot of foolishness. Some of the children don't care if their work is done on time or not. Charles Byler, Ted Horst, and Tyler Zimmerman are all in Brother Brian's room, and their poor attitude sifts down through the rest of the classroom."

"The clique again," said Edna. "I had hoped the three families that banded with the Heiseys would melt back into the congregation again after the Heiseys left. But it's still with us."

"Yes, still with us," said John. "And when a child from one family is punished at school, all three families rise to his defense."

"Is Brother Edward allowing the board to move ahead?"

"A little more," said John. "We still don't get the leverage we need. But any discipline that the board and ministry uphold together tends to cut the proud spirit we are dealing with. Could you make me some tea, please, Edna?"

With a prayer in her heart, Edna put the teapot on to boil.

On Saturday, John came in the door with a grave expression on his face.

"Edna!" he called, "where are you?"

"I'm upstairs changing sheets, John."

"All right. I'll be there," John called back.

"How is the swing coming?" Edna asked brightly as John appeared at the head of the steps. "The children will have so much fun out there, now that spring is coming again!"

"We're making progress," John answered, smiling down at Paul. "I have a really good helper!"

Paul, holding his hammer, beamed into his father's face.

"Did you want something?" asked Edna, scooping an unhappy Conrad from the floor.

"Yes. Brother Edward called with a hot-line prayer request. Rosalie Zimmerman is missing."

"What?" gasped Edna. "Missing? For how long?"

"When Rosalie didn't come to the breakfast table this morning, they went to her bedroom. But she wasn't there. They don't know what happened. Andrew wonders if Trent has anything to do with it. There were no signs of violence."

"Do Trent and Rosalie still have a friendship?" asked Edna. "I thought Andrew told Rosalie she had to quit seeing Trent, a little before he left Meadow Brook."

"That's right," said John. "They're wondering if that had something to do with it."

"Did she take anything along?" asked Edna.

"Yes," said John. "Most of her clothing and personal things are still there. But Rosalie's important legal papers, like her birth certificate, are missing from the office. She just turned eighteen yesterday."

"Oh, no," said Edna. "I hope she doesn't make a rash decision to marry Trent and then regret it for the rest of her life."

"The police are looking for her," said John. "We're gathering at the church to pray at eleven o'clock this morning. How soon can we be ready?"

Edna moved through the afternoon with a heavy sense of dread and sadness. Missing? What a terrible word to apply to Rosalie. Was she safe?

The phone rang at suppertime. John jumped at the sound, overturning his water cup. But neither he nor Edna noticed.

"Hello?" he queried.

Edna listened intently to the one-sided conversation.

"Yes? . . . Oh, no! Are they sure? . . . What can we do? . . . Well, we'll keep on praying."

John laid down the phone with a dull look in his eyes.

"Rosalie called home at two o'clock this afternoon and told Nettie that she and Trent are getting married. Andrew got on the phone and told Rosalie that the police are looking for her and that he needed to know if she was safe. She said she was. Later this afternoon, the police caught up with the pair and had an interview with them. There was really nothing the police could do except make sure Rosalie wasn't being kidnapped. She is eighteen."

Edna went to the bedroom and cried into her pillow.

"John," she said brokenly, when he entered the bedroom, "if Andrew's had helped Rosalie do right, instead of defending her when she did wrong, and if Brother Edward had addressed problems in the Zimmerman family and in Trent's life as they occurred, would this have happened? No one in authority really tried to stop the young people from doing wrong."

"I know, Edna. I know," said John. "It breaks my heart. But it is just like the Bible says in Proverbs 29:15: 'The rod and reproof give wisdom: but a child left to himself bringeth his mother to shame.' "

"May God help us to be faithful with our children!" Edna said fervently, rising from the bed and patting her hair into place. "Right now I hear them needing me at the table. Is there anything we should do for Andrew's?"

"Maybe we'll go over to see Andrew and Nettie tomorrow, to let them know we care. Moses said the ministry is with them today," answered John.

CHAPTER 17

"Mama," called Rachel as she ran to the garden. "Here is our letter from Grandma! May I open it? If Grandma answered my letter, can Paul keep on watching the little ones while I read?"

Edna stood up from the beet row, her hands full of beets. "Yes, that will be fine," she said. "Then after about five minutes, tell Paul to come out and help me while you watch the children again."

Edna hummed as she finished pulling the beets. Tonight was John's twenty-ninth birthday, and she and the children were making plans. John had chosen roast beef, mashed potatoes, gravy, and green beans for his birthday supper.

"Mama," Paul called from the kitchen window. "Conrad won't listen to me."

"I'm coming," answered Edna, lifting the dishpan of beets.

After order was restored, Edna called all the children

around her. "Now, what kind of dessert do you think Daddy would like?"

"Cherry pie," said Paul.

"Carrot cake," said Rachel. "Daddy likes carrot cake a lot."

"I like banana cake!" Hannah said, leaning onto her mother's lap.

Edna smiled. "You all have such good ideas that I'm not sure which one to choose. But I did hear Daddy saying he's hungry for cherry pie, so we'll make that. Now, I need each of you bigger ones to make a nice card for Daddy's birthday. Rachel, you can help the little ones."

Taking the opened envelope from the desk, Edna settled into the rocking chair to read her mother's letter.

"Dear Edna," she read. "I greet you in Jesus' Name. I have such a longing to come over and take all the little ones onto my lap again. I have an idea that Father will soon tell me that I can come over for an afternoon again. I love you all!

"I'm a little worried about Father. You know how he has always been robust and hearty, even longer than most other men his age. Lately he tires so easily. I don't know if it's simply because he's almost sixty, or if something else is wrong. I also think he looks a little pale sometimes. So I just wanted you to know.

"I know you long to have contact with Father, like we talked about the last time I came over. But rest assured that the letters you write also reach him. Father reads them in my presence now. He often gets one out of the drawer to reread before he crawls into bed at night."

Edna laid the letter in her lap, pondering. Could Father be sick? Was he ready to die? Edna sighed. Then she smiled as another thought struck her. Did the Spirit of God place it there? In her letters she would write about the sermons she had heard and the thoughts that had come to her mind. Then God could direct those thoughts to reach her father's heart. "Lord," Edna prayed, "You know all about my father and how much I long for him to be saved. Please speak to him so he will come to repentance before he dies. Use me to touch him, Lord," she finished.

"Good-bye, Edna," John called as he hurried out the door after lunch on Saturday. "Steve says we'll probably be back from passing out literature by about four o'clock this afternoon. If all the young people show up, it usually takes about an hour and a half to cover the route we use in town."

Edna waved as John pulled out the driveway. As she finished the cleaning and cared for the children, she often thought of the group in town. "Lord," she prayed, "bless the seed of your Word as it falls into the hearts of men. Be with John, and give him what he needs."

Arriving at church, John began counting out tracts while Brother Steve organized groups. "We'll help you, John," Melvin Kauffman offered as he and Doreen came over to the back bench. Gradually more of the young people drifted over to help.

"Thank you," said John. "Here, Brian. Would you please take this box out to Brother Moses' van? And, Kent, could you put this box in Brother Steve's van, please?"

"Sure," answered Brian, while Kent nodded.

"Now," said Brother Steve, "we'll number off. We'll count off one, two, one, two around the circle. Group one will go in Brother Moses' van. The rest will go with me."

John hopped into the driver's seat of Brother Moses' van and looked into the rear-view mirror. Brother Steve's plan had been a good idea. His group held a mixed cross section of the group. The casual dress some of the young people wore bothered him. But what could he do?

"Let's sing," said John. "We'll start with 'Send the Light.'"

Music floated through the van. When the tenor faltered, John looked back and noticed that Brian and Howard were not singing. Instead, they were throwing spitballs at each other. Question marks began to form in his mind. He would have to split the boys up today.

John stopped at the first street of Quail Run Development.

"Regina and Annette," he said, "you two can take the right-hand side of the street. Caleb and Brian, you take the left-hand side of the street. Stay fairly close to the girls, in case they need any help. Then move over to the next street. Howard and I will be on Spelding Boulevard, the third one down."

"Got stuck with Young Preacher," John heard Brian mutter to Howard as he got out of the van.

"And I'm stuck with Old Preacher," Howard whispered back. "We'll have to walk straight."

At Spelding, John parked the van, and he and Howard got out. John chatted pleasantly with Howard as they took the same side of the street, getting alternate houses.

Halfway up the other side, John looked up to see some of the group waiting near the van. What was Brian doing? Was he making airplanes out of tracts and doing target practice on the shrubs at the first house? Surely not! But as John came closer, he saw that Brian was.

At that moment the house door opened, and an irate man stepped out.

"I'll have you know I won't have you putting rubbish in my yard!" he said in a cold, controlled voice. "I work hard to keep this place nice. And I don't need any religion from people who don't respect the property of others. Get out, young man!"

Brian gasped and quickly hurried back to the van, his face flaming. He tried the door, only to find it locked.

John stepped up to the property owner.

"Sir," he said, "you have every right to be disappointed. I am too. We'll make sure this doesn't happen again. May I clean up the mess for you?"

The irate man looked at John levelly. "I'm sorry," he said. "I've been taking heat all day. I'm a police officer, and I work with juvenile delinquents. And then to see a Mennonite lad, who should know better, trashing up my yard—while he's peddling religion—blew my stack.

"Young man," he said, turning to Brian, "you have one of the best opportunities in the world. You probably have a family that cares about you and tries to teach you how to live. Most young people today aren't that fortunate. Listen, you straighten out your act." He paused and began again, with a touch of gentleness. "Now, lad, you come back here and clean up the mess yourself."

Brian came awkwardly forward and retrieved the paper jets. But he said nothing. "Brian," John said quietly, "you should apologize."

"I'm sorry, sir," Brian managed to say. "I won't do it again."

"Mister," John said in parting as he held out his hand, "my name is John Troyer. Again, I apologize."

The officer shook John's hand and then went back into the house.

A quiet group rode home in the van.

"Young people," John began, "you see what inconsistency can do to our Christian testimony. Let's each make a commitment with our lives that we will live what God teaches in the Bible.

"Sometimes foolish things we feel like doing seem so innocent to us, but life is largely made up of little things that make the whole. Our outlook needs to be serious, and our lives need to be committed to God. Then our lives will be a living testimony that honors God.

"We should handle property in a respectful way," John continued, "whether that property is tracts that have a sacred message from God, or the lawns of other people."

Most of the young people were nodding in agreement as John looked into their faces in the rear-view mirror. The air had been cleared, and most of them relaxed. "We'll sing again," he said pleasantly. "Any selections?"

Soon music wafted through the van. Brian and Howard were subdued. No paper wads flew through the air on the way home. And though the tenor was a bit soft, there were no lapses.

Edna settled beside John on the couch. A full moon glistened in the frame of the windowpane. "How did your afternoon go?" she asked. "I was praying for you while you were gone."

"Thank you, Edna. I knew you would be praying. Most of the afternoon went well. I did have one sticky situation to handle. One of the boys disturbed a gentleman by littering his yard."

Edna frowned as John recounted the story. "Really, John?" she asked. "With tracts?"

"Yes. Brother Steve and I talked about it afterward. Brother Steve told me to call Andrew and tell him what happened. He said he would share the situation with Brother Edward."

"I've noticed that Brother Edward takes Brother Steve fairly seriously," said Edna.

"Yes," said John, "he does."

"How did your phone call to Andrew go?"

"I didn't call," said John. "I stopped in before I came home. Andrew was surprised to hear what had happened. He seemed to believe what I told him, though he did say that he would ask Brian about it.

"One thing I am sure of," John added, "and that is that Brian will not do target practice on Spelding Boulevard again. Today a property owner made him accountable by calling him on the carpet. He sobered him, by bringing law into his life."

Edna frowned. "If only his parents would do that! It's sad that one or two people can spoil things for a whole group. I think you did a good job of handling things, John, and I hope you were able to undo some of the damage Brian did. But just think how this foolishness dimmed the testimony of our church in the officer's mind."

John nodded. "I know. It is a serious matter. Brother Steve suggested it might be wise to screen who can go along the next time."

"Would Brother Edward be willing to do that?"

"I don't know," answered John. "Perhaps if Brother Steve suggests it."

CHAPTER 18

"Edna," asked John one Sunday afternoon, "would you like to go over to see Moses and Sally this evening?"

"Sure," said Edna. "I have a baby gift ready to go. I'm eager to hold little Abigail."

"If I help you with the dishes, we should have everybody ready to leave by six-thirty. That way we can have time to talk and still leave in good time to settle our families for the night.

"Moses and I have become really good friends, besides being brothers in Christ," said John. "I'd like to let him know some of the thoughts we're thinking about church life and see what he says."

Edna nodded. "I understand. Sally and I can look after the children while you talk."

The house rang with the happy chatter of children that evening. Edna smiled into Abigail's tiny face as she rocked the baby to sleep and watched her own children play in the dining room. It was good to have an evening with Sally. Moses and John withdrew to a quiet corner of the living room.

"Have you finished harvesting corn for this fall?" asked John.

"Almost," answered Moses. "All my own is done. But I have one hundred acres to harvest for a neighbor. And how is work going at the cabinet shop?"

Soon the conversation drifted to less trivial things.

"Moses," John asked, "I want to know what you really think. Edna and I are troubled about the problems that remain in our congregation. You know how conservative issues like the holy kiss; wearing plain coats and simple, plain clothing; music; real integrity; and a serious attitude toward life are slipping.

"I expect problems to come up in church life, but it's what you do with them that determines where your congregation will go spiritually. It troubles me that Brother Edward is often the one who blocks attempts to deal with issues. Then what can concerned members do? Are we warranted in seeking another fellowship? Please be honest with me," John finished.

Brother Moses nodded meditatively. For a moment he closed his eyes, as if in prayer. Then he opened them and looked at John.

"John," he said, "I hadn't intended to tell you quite yet, but I would have told you soon anyway. Sally and I are planning to leave Meadow Brook."

John started.

"I have been running into the problem of working with

Brother Edward's lenient views ever since I was ordained. It worked much better when our families were almost all supportive. But you know what has happened here in the last three years.

"Sally and I are at the point where we can't keep on going like this much longer. The stress is wearing on both of us, and our children are getting old enough that it is becoming highly important to have a stable setting.

"If I could be effective here, I would be willing to stay," said Moses. "But I can't be effective unless Brother Edward is willing to let law come into the picture. And you know how he tries to avoid that."

John sighed deeply and nodded.

Moses continued. "People who want the liberty to do as they please talk about having spiritual freedom," he said. "But when our hearts are carnal and we do as we please, we have anything but spiritual freedom. Instead we walk into sin in the guise of a religious experience."

"I've been studying the substance of Christianity in my personal devotions," offered John. "I'm impressed with the way we can never separate the condition of our hearts from the way we live. In John 14:23, Jesus says, 'If a man love me, he will keep my words: and my Father will love him, and we will come unto him, and make our abode with him.'

"If Christ is in our hearts, we will keep God's Law—or Jesus' words, as the verse here expresses it. Then Jesus goes on to say that that is the condition for a reciprocating relationship with God and the necessary condition for God to dwell with us."

"Yes," said Moses, "the blood of Jesus Christ cleanses

us from sin." He smiled. "Then Christ issues from our hearts into holy living. I was reading 1 Peter 1:16 this morning. 'Be ye holy; for I am holy.' But you know, John, I can't think of a more beautiful freedom than that. To be godly is to be like God. I can't comprehend the total package of truth and beauty that God is, but I love the glimpses that I get!"

John nodded vigorously. "Lately I read another article that used the terminology of form and content," he said. "The content of our heart must be cleansed and filled with the Spirit of God. Then form—or the way we live—must follow as surely as fragrance comes from a gardenia. And a gardenia smells like a gardenia simply because it is one. Because that's the way gardenias are.

"The article went on to stress that our heart content and our form must come together in harmony, if we are real. You would never expect a gardenia to smell like a pigpen."

"Well, no, I guess you wouldn't." Moses smiled. Then he sobered. "But we do the same thing if we try to separate the way we live from our heart condition."

"What do you think about the broad-based objection to imposing our culture on other people who become Christians?" asked John.

"Well," said Moses, "the dictionary definition of *culture* simply says it is the way we do things. So will we have a Christian culture if we are 'little Christs'? By all means we will. Then the way we do things will be the way Christ would do them—and our guidelines to do that are found in the Bible. We can't avoid culture. It's going to be a part of us, no matter what course we choose to follow.

It is true that there are some differences in applications, but that thought is being stretched today to justify losing principles," Moses finished.

"What we starve dies," John said thoughtfully, "and what we feed grows. The more we open our hearts up to God, the more we will grow into Him."

"Amen!" seconded Moses. He sat quietly for a few minutes.

"John," he said, rousing from his reverie, "never forget this. We must have a heart after God. Our perspective of God makes a difference as to whether we have revival in our hearts and are tuned to God in a spiritual experience. The narrow way of obedience is not a difficult way. It is the way to freedom."

John nodded vigorously. "You are right, Moses," he said. "It is. And when I count the cost of doing God's will or my own, what I really should be thinking of is the dreadful cost of not taking God's way."

"We're back to the vine again," said Moses. "We cannot have the life of Christ within us unless we abide in the vine—and then His life flows out through our lives.

"To walk with God is to know the joy of eternity. Then the strength of the vine flows into us and leads us into spiritual places a carnal mind cannot comprehend."

"Where are you going from here, Moses?"

"We're looking at small outreach churches that need help," answered Moses. "At this point we're seeking God's will about moving to a small church in Wyoming that is asking for help."

"And your prosperous farm here, Moses? What of

that?" asked John, with raised eyebrows.

Moses smiled. "It's going to burn up sometime anyway." He paused and then continued, "We're planning to sell the farm. When we pay off our debt, we should have funds left to buy a place with enough land to keep the children busy. The economy isn't very good in Wyoming. So I may have to drive a distance to find work. But if God wants us to go, He will take care of all that."

"I knew you would say that," said John. "I'm sure God will provide. We'll be praying about your move."

"Thank you. How soon will you be making your decision?"

"Probably in the next few months."

Just before suppertime, the phone rang. It was James.

"Edna," he said, "we just lost a little boy. Denise and I are here in the hospital now, and Denise is wondering if you could come in this evening. She's feeling lonely and needs some encouragement. The nurses don't stay in the room very long, and Denise needs to talk to a woman."

"I'll be happy to come," answered Edna. "I'm so sorry this happened. John should be home soon, and we'll be in as soon as we can."

An hour later the family was in the van, heading to Grandfather Troyer's. Edna waved to the little faces watching from the window as she and John left for the hospital.

Tears filled Edna's eyes as they approached Denise's room. How much James and Denise had been looking forward to this tiny life!

Denise looked up expectantly as Edna entered her

room. "I'm so sorry," Edna murmured as she took Denise's outstretched hand. For a few minutes there were no words, but their tears flowed together.

"What happened, Denise?" Edna finally asked.

"We lost the heartbeat shortly before our little James was born. And by the time he was born, his spirit had already gone to heaven. Little James won't miss anything, but I long for him so much!" Denise sobbed again. "James bears the grief so bravely. But this was his son, Edna, and he really wanted him."

"I'm sure you both did," said Edna. "I know it is a tremendous loss now. But someday you can go to him."

"Yes." Denise smiled slightly. "Like David, we can go to our son."

James slipped quietly into the room.

"Are you ready for John to come in now, Denise?" he asked. "He's out here in the hall."

"Yes," answered Denise.

John and Edna listened quietly as James and Denise shared the events of the day, their struggles, and their hope in Christ in their sorrow.

"John," asked James, "could you please read John 14 to us? We both love that chapter so much."

" 'Let not your heart be troubled,' " read John. " 'Ye believe in God, believe also in me.' "

A holy peace filled the room as weeping hearts sought God.

CHAPTER 19

Brother Edward stood up at the close of the service, dark circles showing under his eyes. "Brother Moses has something to share with us," he said.

Brother Moses stood quietly in front of the pulpit for a moment before he spoke. "I have something to share with you this morning that tears my heart," he began. "We have come to love you all, but Sally and I believe that God is leading us to leave the congregation here. We plan to be working with a little mission church in Wyoming.

"As we leave, I beg you all to be faithful to God and to beware of apostasy. Follow God's Word and die daily to self in your lives. Then God will be honored and you will be blessed. It is our prayer that we will also do the same thing."

The auditorium was deathly still as Brother Moses sat down.

Edna sat with bowed head, weeping softly. Why must there be so much sorrow in life?

"Edna," asked John as he prepared to leave for work, "would it suit you to take my check in to the bank this morning? Abner said we can pick it up this morning."

"I'll do that when I take Rachel and Paul to school," Edna offered. "Doreen will be here. She can keep the younger children until I get back. I need a few groceries in town anyway. I should be back in an hour."

Edna waved to Rachel and Paul as she drove out of the school yard. They waved back, Paul hugging his new lunch box, and hurried into the building. Another school year was starting.

In a few minutes, Edna arrived at the shop office.

"Hello," Abner greeted her as she entered the office. "John is out installing today. You came for a check, right?"

"Hello," answered Edna. "Yes, we would appreciate picking it up today if we could."

"Emma does the payroll," Abner explained, "and she hasn't brought the checks out yet. You're welcome to go into the house. I think she has them finished."

Edna walked up to the house. Emma's flower beds were still beautiful! She knocked on the door. One of the children answered.

"Did you want Mom?" Gabriel asked. "Come in. I'll get her from the basement."

Edna walked into the living room, surprised at the music that was coming from somewhere. In a few moments the basement door opened and Emma appeared. She looked in surprise at the children.

"Who turned that radio program on?" she asked. "Daddy doesn't let you listen to that."

"Elam did," said Gabriel.

"Did you, Elam?"

"Yes." The boy hung his head.

"Go to Daddy's office and stay there until I come," Emma said sternly.

Emma turned to Edna. "Now, welcome, Edna!" she said. "Gabriel and Elizabeth, you can play as soon as your beds are made." She drew out a chair for Edna.

"I'm so glad to see you," Emma said. "How are things going?"

"We're doing well," said Edna. She paused. Should she tell Emma more? Edna hesitated, then continued.

"Actually we're feeling a little burdened right now," said Edna. "We're concerned about the drift that is taking place at Meadow Brook. I tell you that because you are my friend."

Emma nodded thoughtfully. "I'm glad you were honest with me. And I'm wondering if I would dare to be honest with you?"

"I'll be glad to hear anything you have to share," Edna said reassuringly.

"I know I can trust you, and I desperately need to talk to someone. Edna, things aren't going well spiritually for our family, and I hardly know what to do. You see the dress I'm wearing. It doesn't have a cape, because Abner doesn't want me to wear one anymore. For a long time I held out to wear a cape, because I want myself and my girls to dress modestly. But that went like so many other issues go.

"Abner doesn't say I absolutely have to give up the

things we both thought were important at one time. But he tells me that we are placing our salvation in those things and wants me to pray about whether God is really telling me to do what I'm doing. Then he puts emotional pressure on me until I end up doing what he wants me to do. It's one thing after another, Edna. I don't like what's happening to me or the children."

Edna's gaze drew in the evidences around the home, and she nodded her head. "I'm sure that's hard, Emma. I know you want to be a submissive wife and that you also want to do what's right."

"Exactly," said Emma. "At Living Waters, they teach that a woman should do what her husband wants her to do unless that deed is entirely wrong. So I thought, is it possible to be modest without a cape? I decided it was and made a very loose dress. But then the girls don't make theirs the same way. What Abner is satisfied with for them doesn't seem modest to me. We're slipping, Edna, and I don't know what to do!" Emma cried softly.

"We'll pray for you, Emma. But remember, you never have to do anything wrong to please anyone. We must honor our husbands, but we must honor God and His Word more. Be faithful, and God will be with you in every hard circumstance."

Emma swallowed her sobs and squeezed Edna's hand.

Edna's heart wept as she left the distraught woman. What could she do for Emma?

It was only when she was about to start the minivan that she remembered that she had come for a check. Quickly she retraced her steps to the door.

"John," said Edna, "it really tears me up. What should a woman like Emma do?"

"That's a hard situation," John said. "I know what she's talking about because I see Abner's family around the shop. But a woman finally has to do what is right, even if her husband objects. In Emma's case, it will take a lot of wisdom to know what to do in each situation. We must pray for her! I hadn't realized she feels this way."

"I often wonder why a man like Abner went wrong, John," said Edna. "I don't think I ever saw a man who had stronger intentions to do what was right when we and Abner's and James were seeking God's will together."

"I know what you mean," said John. "When we were having our Bible studies, Abner taught me a lot of things and strengthened my faith many times. But he made one major mistake. He believed something that wasn't true.

"We give the devil strongholds in our lives when we operate from the basis of beliefs that aren't truth. When we adopt a platform that isn't true, we give the devil that space in our lives to build on. Then he has a base for operation, and he deceives us."

John scratched his head and continued, "You know how we felt when we left Shady Glen, Edna. We wanted to be free from legalism. Well, Abner felt the same way. And in his search for real freedom in Christ, he failed to realize that you could not have content without form. Intending to do the right thing in our hearts does not take care of everything, because the old man in our hearts is still bent on going wrong. We do not naturally do the right thing, even after the Spirit of God is within us. As we choose to do right, we must embrace wisdom from God and His Word and die daily to our carnal desires—or we will make a U-turn away from God."

"What do you mean by saying we can't have content without form?" asked Edna.

"That's just a way of saying you can't have a changed heart without living that way," answered John. "The content of our heart must be pure, and the form—or the way we live—must also be pure. That takes place because the Spirit of God moves and works in us. But it also becomes a matter of choosing to do the right things and crucifying our flesh."

Edna nodded. "I'm glad your father helped us to see that when we left Shady Glen. No wonder our parents were concerned that we could lose out," Edna said soberly, shaking her head.

John nodded. "I also think Abner has gotten caught up in emotionalism. If he has peace and things *feel* good to him, he believes that is God's way of showing him that the thing he is considering is right. When we operate that way, we limit God to what we perceive Him and His Word to be, rather than following the Word itself. We live by the ebb and flow of our feelings, rather than using the Bible as our guide. But the Bible never changes, and it always leads us to know more about God."

"I was thinking of it this way," said Edna. "You know how it is when a pond is freezing over. We can truly believe the ice is thick enough and walk fearlessly onto the pond. But whether we will be safe on the ice has nothing to do with the way we *feel* about the ice. The absolutes—whether the ice is thick enough—determine if we go through the ice or not."

"Exactly," said John, "and what God says about something is our absolute."

"How do you think Moses and Sally are doing now?" queried Edna.

"Moses said it's harder to leave than they thought it would be, but he believes they're doing the right thing. You know how disappointed and torn up the congregation is."

Edna nodded. "I understand, because for all the concerned families in our congregation, this is a *huge* loss."

"Shall we give our cares to God and go to bed?" asked John.

Edna yawned and agreed.

Chapter 20

"Here, John," said Edna. "Could you sharpen these knives for me, please?"

"Sure," said John. "We'll need some sharp ones to butcher with today. Father's hog is just about as big as ours is. And ours is big! I looked at him when I did chores this morning. He must weigh about 250 pounds. So we will be processing a lot of meat. Can Doreen help today?"

"She can come at nine," answered Edna. "We'll be glad for her."

"Father and Mother should be here anytime," said John. "We'll let you and Mother know when we're ready for you ladies. I have the worktables set up in the back yard like we usually do, so you can keep some of the worst mess out of the house."

"Good," said Edna. "The temperature is about right today—cold enough to butcher safely, but not cold enough to freeze us out. And fairly bright for a November day."

John nodded and looked out the window. "Here comes Lady!" he said. "You'll have to feed her a carrot today, Edna."

"I will. What about you?"

John smiled. "Oh, I've already put a lump of brown sugar in my pocket. We can't forget a good horse like Lady."

Lady whinnied as John walked up to unhitch her. Edna watched as John stroked her nose. Then he held out his hand with something in it. Lady quickly claimed the sugar lump.

"Oh, Grandmother!" exclaimed Rachel as she welcomed Grace. "I'm glad today is Saturday so I can be here when you come!"

Grace laughed. "And so am I, Rachel! This is going to be a busy, happy day."

"Mama said it will be Paul's job and mine to keep the little children happy."

Grace smiled. "Yes, I know you are a good helper. Just think—you're eight now, Rachel. Paul is six and in first grade already!"

Grace turned to Edna. "It makes me think of the time when all of our children were little," she said, smiling. "It was a busy, busy time, but it was one of the happiest periods of my life."

Hannah and Mary both came with a book. "Read to us, Grandmother!" begged Hannah.

"One book for each of you," said Grace, "and I'll show a book to Conrad." She picked the toddler up from the floor. "Then we will look forward to reading again this afternoon."

After the children were settled into their play, Edna and Grace worked companionably in the kitchen, washing up the breakfast dishes and preparing food for the day.

"Edna," said Grace, "I wish you could see your father. Did Mary tell you he isn't well?"

Edna looked up sharply from the pudding she was stirring. "Yes. Mother still writes to me every week, and she often tells me that Father isn't doing well. Is it worse than I know?"

"I'm not sure," said Grace, "but he doesn't look like a well man, and it concerns me. Edna, does your father know the Lord?"

Edna sighed. "I don't know. Father has always been a good, honest man. But he doesn't have the interests of a man who really knows God.

"I know he reads the letters I write home each week. So John and I have both been sharing tidbits of messages and thoughts that we have—hoping that they will be able to touch Father in some way."

"He reads your letters?" Grace raised her eyebrows.

"Yes," Edna said. "Father won't talk to me or wave to me when we happen to pass on the road, and I can't go home. But Mother says he reads our letters every night. So I always remember that when I am writing. God has still given me a channel to reach my father, and I am so glad!"

The door opened and John, Sr., stuck his head in the door. "We're ready for you, Mother and Edna."

After a few instructions to Rachel and Paul, Edna bundled up and headed out to the worktables. While John and his father used the meat saws to make cuts, Edna's and

Grace's knives flew deftly as they took the meat off the bones.

"Have you heard from the other children lately?" John asked his father.

"We got letters from Edgar's and Henry's yesterday," said John, Sr. "Sadie and Florence stopped in the other night."

"How is Edgar's house coming?" asked John.

"They said they're about ready to put the roof on now," John, Sr., answered. "I wish I could help," he said. "But my hip isn't good enough for that anymore."

"Do you think Edgar would feel comfortable if I would go for a few days to help?" asked John.

John, Sr., shook his head. "Not likely," he answered.

John sighed. "Well," he said, "you and Mother can't know how much it means to us that you haven't been afraid to associate with us since we belong to the Meadow Brook Mennonite Church. We can't have much to do with Edna's siblings either. So being welcome at your house means a lot to us."

"How are things going at Meadow Brook since Moses and Sally left last month?" asked John, Sr.

"Well," said John, "not that much has really changed, other than the big hole we feel since Moses' family isn't there. Moses saw issues the way they were, and he and Sally were always in touch with the congregation, meeting needs. The concerned families feel distressed to have lost a leader with conviction, but the other families don't appear to be affected."

"And you?"

"If things don't improve," answered John, "Edna and I are at the point of making a change too. Too much conviction has been lost, and careless attitudes are still producing carnality. Too many have a casual attitude toward their spiritual lives. Then that blossoms out in materialism, living for the present, and a tolerant attitude toward sin. The line between the world and the church continues to be clouded."

"So you would say sin is not being dealt with by your leaders?"

"Not to an acceptable degree," said John. "I'm thinking now of what Stephen told us when we left Shady Glen. He said, 'Stick with a church that deals with sin, John.' "

"You're still thinking of Pine Ridge?" asked Grace.

"Yes," said John. "I know there are small churches that need help. But as we pray, we feel the Lord is leading us to stay here in this area. God knows the future, and we want to be in the center of His will."

"Well," said John, Sr., "we want you to follow God's will, and sometimes that is away from parents. But if you stay here, it will mean a lot to Mother and me to have one son in the area that we can depend on. We do feel our age."

"We certainly want to be here for you," John stated firmly.

"We appreciate that," John, Sr., said. "And we appreciate that you are staying faithful to God, instead of losing principles and drifting into the world. Above all, we want our children to know God and to be faithful to Him," he emphasized.

"By the grace of God, we will be faithful," said John.

"Edna and I have often been grateful for the advice you gave us when we left Shady Glen. That has helped us to keep our convictions and our spiritual moorings. You're still satisfied where you are, Mother and Father?"

John, Sr., glanced at Grace. "I don't know, John," he answered. "I've been getting some resistance to passing out tracts. But at this point, we're still staying."

"I always remember you as a faithful man, Father," John said. "But you didn't always have the spiritual interest you've had in the last five to ten years. I know you have said you sought God in a new way, and He answered. But I never really asked you how God led you on that journey."

"Well, it had a lot to do with you, son," answered John, Sr. "I watched a number of you children sow wild oats, and most of you came back and settled down again. It was when you were at your lowest point that the truth gripped me that I really hadn't been offering a real Christianity to my children. Out in the barn one night, as I wept into the straw, praying for you, I asked God to come completely into my life and make me a real blessing to you children— and to mark you for His own.

"I wouldn't say I wasn't saved before that, but things have been different ever since then," answered John, Sr. "God has become more real to me since I made that commitment to Him, and Mother and I pray daily for all of you."

John bowed his head, too moved to talk.

"We're about ready to move inside now," said John. "Can you give me a hand with this tub of sausage meat, Father?"

Edna hurried into the kitchen to cover the table with newspapers. Doreen stood up from the rocker and tiptoed into the bedroom with a sleeping Conrad. The women filled the jars with meat. Soon the gas burner outside and the stove burners were filled to capacity.

"Have you seen Sam lately, John?" asked John, Sr., as he wrapped roasts in freezer paper.

"No," answered John. "But Edna's mother tells us he hasn't been well. The only way we can touch him is through the letters we write to Edna's mother."

"He looks like a very sick man," said John, Sr. "Mother and I are praying that he will let you visit them."

Edna wept into her pillow that night. "Lord," she prayed, "draw my father to Yourself, and use me to bless him."

Then she slipped to her knees beside the bed and remained there for a long time.

CHAPTER 21

Wednesday evening came. Edna pulled a hymnbook from the rack and turned to song number 7. Her eyes scanned the page. She smiled and joined in singing "Oh, Could I Speak the Matchless Worth."

"Lord," she prayed, "I worship You. What a wonderful Father You are. Guide us carefully."

As Edna's eyes swept over the congregation, her heart filled with warmth. Here were the faithful, dedicated members who had been such a blessing to her and John. Then she sighed involuntarily. There was also the faction of members who looked upon church as a social center and who took the liberty to live as they chose. Edna sighed deeply, for she loved them all.

John shared the worship service from the back where he sat with an ailing Conrad. He saw the faithful worshiping reverently. He also noticed the communication and laughter among some of the girls, and the casually dressed young boys who slouched in their seats and chewed gum. Where was the fear of God in their experience?

"Lord," John prayed, "help this congregation to deal with sin so that Your light can shine brightly."

Brother Steve looked weary as he stood up to have devotions. John bowed his head for a moment to ask a special blessing for him from God. A light titter of laughter rippled through the boys on the back seat as Charles Byler passed something down the row.

After prayer, Charles walked up to the podium to have the topic of the evening. "This evening we're going to look at honoring God with our lives," Charles began. "I've been impressed with what the Bible says on the subject. Honoring God needs to touch every area of our lives."

John listened with rapt attention. The topic turned out to be a very good one. But his heart was sickened. Did Charles really mean a thing he had said?

John was reading to the children when the phone rang the next Sunday afternoon. He got up to answer.

"Yes," he said, "I think we can come. Conrad is feeling better, and I'm sure we would all enjoy it. Five-thirty? All right! We'll be there."

"Who?" Edna asked brightly.

"Denise invited us to supper tonight. Do you want to go?"

"Sure!" said Edna. "You still have time to take a nap."

John lay down on the couch, but sleep was slow in coming.

"I can't sleep," he said. "I'd rather just talk instead. What are you thinking about, Edna?"

"I was thinking of the prayer your father prayed for us when we were choosing a church more than four years ago," Edna said. "Somehow that prayer was burned in my memory. He asked God to give us the Spirit of Christ and to lead us surely as we made our decision."

"And we still need that," asserted John. "I also remember that he prayed that God would give us wisdom and understanding, and that if we erred, God would cause us to know and give us hearts that would always obey Him and turn back."

"Do you think we erred in coming to Meadow Brook, John?" asked Edna.

"Sometimes I wonder," answered John. "Things were more Scriptural when we started coming. But if I had been wiser, I would have noticed more things and had a deeper perception of where those things usually lead. I'm sorry, Edna. If I had chosen to go to Pine Ridge four years ago, I could have saved us a lot of stress. And you would have been happy with that decision."

"I don't fault you, John," Edna answered. "You were trying to do the best you knew at the time, and you're ready to do what needs to be done now. I appreciate that."

John smiled and nodded. Then he began to twirl his rooster tail. "I've learned a number of things in the last four years," he said thoughtfully. "I'm wiser now about what it takes to have a pure church. Remember how I was afraid Pine Ridge was too legalistic, Edna?"

"Yes."

"Now I know that church discipline that commands the respect of the church members is a real blessing—not something to be afraid of. The heart issue is important. When we feed carnality, our hearts grow colder. When we feed spiritual interests, our hearts grow toward God. And when we quit reaching for worldly things and chafing to get them, our lives can go on with the fruitfulness the Christian life is all about."

"Oh, I know what you mean," Edna said thoughtfully. "I long for the rest and harmony that comes from everyone quietly doing what God wants him to do."

"Yes," John agreed. "We need to die to self. Then we abide in Christ, while His life flows through us and makes us fruitful. If we abide in Christ, we will keep our eyes upon Him and love and obey Him."

"Who would want the burden of living for himself?" asked Edna. "We have both done that, and it is the most miserable way to live!"

"Exactly," said John, nodding meditatively.

" 'Abide in me, and I in you,' " quoted Edna. " 'As the branch cannot bear fruit of itself, except it abide in the vine; no more can ye, except ye abide in me.' I like John 15:4."

"We'll keep on fasting and praying that God will show us what He wants us to do," said John. "God will be faithful in giving us wisdom."

Edna smiled. "Yes," she said, "and strength to follow His direction."

Edna looked forward to spending the evening with Denise. Her heart saddened as she thought of the little one Denise would not be holding this evening. How much healing had four months brought?

"How is it going, Denise?" asked Edna as she helped with the dishes.

Denise gazed thoughtfully out the kitchen window, where stars sparkled above the white snow. Then she turned and looked at Edna.

"I think we're doing about as good as you can expect to after you lose a little one you've longed for," Denise answered quietly. "James and I feel little James's loss keenly. But we are learning to give him to God and go on. Maybe by spring I'll feel like getting into the garden again."

Edna nodded. "And for now, you're still doing the right thing. You're focusing the right way, and God will be able to turn this loss into a blessing in some way."

Denise shook her head ruefully. "I need to learn to give up again and again," she began. "When I married James, I somehow expected that my sorrow was over and that 'happy days were here again,' like the little song we used to sing when school was out. But in the school of life, God is always teaching us. And we need to bow to God and learn the lessons He wants to teach us and receive the blessings that will come from that. What about you and John?" asked Denise.

"Well," said Edna, "I think we're all right. But we do feel heavy when we think about moving our membership from Meadow Brook. We had planned to stay there. But we want to follow God, and we long for a holy, committed church."

"You know," said Denise, "when I was shopping, a lady

asked me a strange question. First, she asked me if I was a Mennonite. Then she asked, 'Are you from that Mennonite church where the young people can do anything they want to? I have some neighbors who go there, and you wouldn't believe the things they do! I think it's Meadow something.' At first, I hardly knew what to say. Then I just told her that we go to Pine Ridge and that it is our desire to honor God with our whole lives."

Edna shook her head. "May God help us to be faithful!" she exclaimed.

In the living room, John and James settled into comfortable chairs and prepared for a long talk.

"I hear what you're saying," James said as John shared the burden his heart carried. "We've been praying for you.

"I agree with you about the necessity of having a pure church. I don't know of any church that has a consistent practice without having a disciplined body. Otherwise, uncommitted people will come in and spoil the group, or sin rises among people who once meant to do what is right."

"I don't know of any consistent church that doesn't use firm church discipline either," said John. "But God knew that long ago when he instructed Paul to write 1 Corinthians 5. After Paul told them to discipline the sinner in their midst, he wrote, 'Your glorying is not good. Know ye not that a little leaven leaveneth the whole lump? Purge out therefore the old leaven, that ye may be a new lump, as ye are unleavened. For even Christ our passover is sacrificed for us.' "

"When we die to the flesh, we can live to God," James added. "That's true Christian liberty."

"Call me when you need help with anything," offered Denise as the family left. "The children and I need something to do, and it would give us all a breath of fresh air."

"I will," agreed Edna.

Edna looked at the tiny baby she held in her arms. What a blessing Sarah would be!

"John," she asked, a tender smile on her face, "could you call Denise? I'd love to share Sarah with her, and maybe she can help us until Doreen gets here."

"Good idea," said John. "I'll also call our folks' neighbors to tell both of them. Sarah looks just like her mother."

Edna smiled. "Do you think so, John?"

"Yes," John said gently. "But what I care most about is that she has her mother's heart and character."

"We'll give her to God and do the best we can, John," Edna said, cradling the tiny girl.

Denise came within fifteen minutes.

"I left the children with my sister," she said. "James doesn't care how long I stay."

"Do you want her?" Edna asked, holding the baby toward Denise.

Denise took the baby quietly and began to rock her. A few tears coursed down her cheeks. Then she began to sing softly to little Sarah.

Edna turned her head the other way to give Denise her own space.

Sarah was one week old when Edna looked out the window in surprise. Her mother was coming in the lane at a rapid pace. As she approached the door, her face looked gray.

"Mother!" Edna exclaimed. "What is it?"

Mary sat down on the rocker Edna offered her and cried. "It's Father," she said. "He has cancer."

Edna's face turned white. "Really?" she gasped.

"Yes," Mary continued between her sobs. "We were both afraid this was coming. But when you know for sure . . . I guess you're never ready. The doctor thinks Father could live a year or two with treatment."

"Oh, I wish I could see my father!" exclaimed Edna.

"There is one good thing in this," said Mary. "Father said he might let you come home again. He wants to see his daughter before he dies."

Edna bowed her head and cried again. Why must joy be so intertwined with sorrow?

Two weeks later John and Edna asked for membership at Pine Ridge and began attending there. The congregation welcomed them with open arms. Edna's heart warmed as she shared in the fellowship and drank in the services. Her heart was at rest.

"I feel that I have come home again, John," said Edna. "People are so kind to us. I don't feel that we deserve this."

"No, I guess we don't," said John. "But we don't deserve anything good. Blessings all come from the mercy of God, and He loves to bless us! And He often blesses us through His people."

Edna nodded thoughtfully.

CHAPTER 22

Edna rocked Sarah gently as she looked around the living room walls of Emily Troyer's home. Voices drifted in from the dining room, where some of the church sisters were stitching comforters together. At last the baby's eyes closed, and she was sleeping soundly. Edna laid Sarah on one of the makeshift beds on the floor in Rodney and Emily's bedroom. "What shall I do?" she asked Rose Miller when she returned to the dining room.

"We're just about done knotting this comforter," answered Rose. "Would you mind sewing a little dress together?"

Edna picked up a soft pink print from the stack of cut-out dresses and placed her sewing machine on one of the worktables. For a moment, her eyes followed Rose. Her hair was almost silver, but the face it framed was so gentle that the wrinkles almost seemed to melt away. There was something unfathomable in the caring brown eyes. What a blessing the deacon's wife was becoming in her life! Rose moved about the room, directing a number of projects. She stopped to peer over Edna's shoulder.

"I have been wondering how things are going with your father," Rose said quietly.

Edna laid down the unfinished bodice and turned around to answer. "My father is getting a little stronger, though they say he's still in bed most of the time. The round of chemotherapy they tried was finished two months ago. The tumor has shrunk, and he's feeling better now that the treatments are over."

"I'm glad to hear that," Rose said sincerely. "And has he allowed you to come home yet?"

"We're going over tonight." Edna's face glowed. "It will be the first time I am home in four and a half years."

"We'll be praying for you," said Rose. "God will give you words to share with Sam. Aaron met him in the hospital when he was visiting a friend. Now Aaron stops in to visit your father sometimes. He said Sam seems like a noble man."

"I didn't know that!" Edna exclaimed. "I have been asking God to send someone who can talk to him. My father has not been a careless man, but I long so much that he will come to know the Lord before he dies."

Emily looked up from her sewing machine. "We're all praying for that, Edna," she added.

Edna's heart beat rapidly as she and John got the little ones out of their car seats and prepared to enter her parents' home.

"John," Edna exclaimed, "is this real?"

John smiled. "I think so. Do you see your mother watching from the window?"

Edna turned around and waved. Then she laughed with a catch in her voice. "Mother has longed for this day almost as much as I have," she said.

Edna was unprepared for the sight of her father as he rested on the recliner. "Father!" she exclaimed, taking the large, thin hand into her own. How he had changed! His clothes hung on his thin body, and hair was beginning to grow back on the sides of his bald head.

"You've come!" he said, in a voice that lacked the volume of previous days. "Edna, I'm dying, and I wanted to see you again." Then he put his head into his hands and wept.

"Oh, Father, I'm so happy to see you again too!" said Edna. "I think of you and pray for you every day. I haven't forgotten you."

"I should have let you come home before," said Sam. "I'm sorry. I see now that it was the wrong thing to do to keep you away."

"I forgive you, Father," said Edna. "Did you read our letters?"

"Yes," said Sam. "I know what has been happening in your life. I see that Rachel and Paul and Hannah have been growing! I want to see the youngest children."

John lifted up Mary, Conrad, and Sarah by turn. Sam reached out to touch each one. Then he leaned back against his pillow and smiled.

Quietly John took the little ones into the kitchen to play.

"How are you, Father?" Edna asked softly.

"Not so good, Edna," Sam answered. "The doctor says I might have a year if I go through all the treatments. But it's hardly worth it to go through more chemotherapy, when I know it will only gain me a little more time—and still be wretched."

Mary adjusted Sam's pillows and offered him a drink. "Do you care what we decide to do about more treatments, Edna?" asked Mary.

"I think that's for Father to decide," Edna answered quietly. "Is there really no hope?"

"No," Sam said. "Only a little more time, which might all be spent in this recliner."

"It's only this, Father," Edna continued. "I can't bear to see you die without knowing that you have received Jesus as your Lord and Saviour. Are you ready to go, Father?" she asked.

"I lie here and think about that every day, Edna," Sam answered. "I thought I tried to please God my whole life. But now I read my Bible and begin to see things I never knew were there. There is a lot that I don't understand. Then I think about the things you and John wrote in the letters, and I know that trying to live a good life will not be enough when my time comes to go."

Edna's breath caught in her throat. "This is my favorite verse, Father," she said. "First John 1:7 tells us, 'The blood of Jesus Christ his Son cleanseth us from all sin.'"

"He was the Lamb of God," Sam said softly, "the perfect sacrifice, as we hear every Communion."

"Yes," said Edna. "He died to bear the sin of the world. When we repent and give our lives to God, He cleanses us with His blood—and our names are written in heaven."

"That's what Aaron Miller said," Sam said. "But I can't quite put it all together."

"Would you like if John or Brother Aaron would have some short Bible studies with you to answer those questions?" asked Edna.

"Yes," said Sam. "Why don't they both come?"

Brother Aaron began meeting with Sam the next day. John also stopped in frequently to spend a short time with him. Together they worked through a Bible course on salvation.

"Dear Lord," prayed Brother Aaron at prayer meeting, "we pray for Sam Yoder. You see his seeking heart. Yet something holds him back. We pray that You will open the doors of his heart and mind so that he will be ready to make a commitment to You."

As Edna cared lovingly for her father or took care of her little ones at home, a prayer was always in her heart. "Oh, Lord, bring my father to repentance, and save his soul."

Brother Brendon Weaver stood up before the congregation at Pine Ridge. John studied the middle-aged bishop. Brother Brendon's face was gentle. Yet the jaw was firm, and his eyes spoke volumes. And when he preached, John grasped every word to seize their payload of spiritual understanding.

"Brethren and sisters," he said, "we have been thinking for some time that we should ordain another minister here. We are asking for the counsel of the congregation to see how you believe the Lord is leading us. We will take your counsel in two weeks.

"We ask everyone to make this a matter of prayer. Unless God leads, we are out of the line of blessing. And we want the full gift and blessing of God."

"John," said Edna, on the way home, "who do you think would be a good minister?"

"Well," said John, "I believe our brethren are sincere, and we don't really have any families that aren't supporting the church."

"That's such a blessing," said Edna. "You wouldn't really want to come to Pine Ridge if you weren't serious about God, because you wouldn't fit. And if you didn't want to support things, . . . I guess you wouldn't be allowed to be a member."

"Yes, that's the blessing of a disciplined fellowship," said John. "As far as candidates go, Levi Mast and Rodney Troyer are both faithful men with leadership abilities."

"What about James?"

John nodded. "I have been thinking of him too."

When the congregational voice was taken, the vote was unanimous.

"Brethren and sisters," Brother Brendon said, "God has spoken to us through the congregation. We will move toward an ordination. We will have the qualification message in four weeks. Then the following Sunday we will take names, with the ordination on the following Wednesday.

"We ask everyone to spend time in prayer and fasting," Brother Brendon continued. "On the Saturday before the nominations are taken, we encourage everyone who can to fast. Then we will meet together to pray that evening."

"John," said Edna as they sat at the table with their tea that night, "I don't know if I ever prayed so much before. Father is always on my heart, and now we have the ordination."

" 'Call unto me, and I will answer thee, and shew thee great and mighty things, which thou knowest not,' " John quoted Jeremiah 33:3.

"I just feel that I need God more every day," Edna said quietly. "It's as if my life is one prayer."

"I think that is the beginning of really growing into God," John answered. "When we feel our need of Him, we are answering the call of God. When we yearn for Him, it is because He first knocked at our doors."

Edna nodded quietly. "Lord," she prayed, "bring my father to know You."

John listened with rapt attention as Brother Brendon stood before the congregation. "We have taken the nominations from the congregation. We have two names, so we will use the lot for the Lord to choose between Brother Rodney and Brother James. Brethren and sisters," he said, "let us be praying."

After church, John moved to talk to both of the brethren. "Brother James," he said as he held James's hand firmly in both of his, "the Lord bless you. We will be praying for you and Denise. Let us know if we can do anything else."

In his mind's eye, John reviewed the course of the last years as his life had interacted with James. There had been the Bible studies in the Shady Glen setting and mutual sharing as he and James had both found their way. Then there had been James's marriage to Denise. And through it all, a rich friendship had continued to grow. James had always been stable. But in the past four or five years, James had developed into a sensitive, godly man with added dimensions.

·James gripped John's hand firmly in turn. There was no need for words.

"The lot has fallen on Brother James." Brother Brendon spoke firmly. "My dear brother, the Lord has called you to be a minister of the Gospel of Jesus Christ. You may rise to answer these questions."

Edna watched as James and Denise stepped forward for James to receive his charge. Edna's heart throbbed with each positive response James intoned during the ceremony.

Her heart was full. James and Denise were closer to her and John than natural brothers or sisters could be. Now they would bless this congregation as the new minister and his wife.

"Lord," prayed Edna, "help us to be strong supporters for James and hold up his hands, as Aaron and Hur helped Moses."

And then Edna prayed the ever-present prayer. "Lord, speak to my father that he may find You as his Saviour."

CHAPTER 23

The cool, fresh days of fall froze in the icy grip of winter. Edna drove gingerly on the slippery roads and looked at the icicles hanging on the house roofs she passed. What a blessing it was to have Doreen to stay with the children. That was another one of the gifts God had given them during this difficult time.

Edna's brow knitted as her thoughts wandered. How much longer would Father live? He had improved since his second round of chemotherapy, but how long would this reprieve last? And when would he find peace for his soul?

"What is troubling you, Father?" John had asked the previous evening.

"I don't know, John," Sam had answered. "I know that I'm not worthy to be saved and that Jesus died to save us. But somehow I can't grasp it."

"We reach out in faith to believe, Father," Edna offered, "just like the snake-bitten Israelites looked up at the brazen serpent on the pole and were healed. It's God's gift to us."

Quietly Edna entered her parents' home. Father was sleeping on his recliner, while Mother napped on the sofa. Softly Edna slipped into the kitchen to fold Father's clean laundry.

"Lord," Edna prayed fervently as her hands smoothed the sheets, "how can we help my father to find You?"

A quiet, forceful thought permeated her mind. "This kind can come forth by nothing, but by prayer and fasting." And a thought kindled. Why not ask the whole church to fast and pray?

"John," said Edna as he set his lunch box on the counter that evening, "something happened to me today. I was asking God how we can help Father find peace, and Mark 9:29 flashed into my mind as well as the thought that our whole church should fast and pray." Edna waited quietly to see what John would say.

He nodded thoughtfully. "That's very Scriptural, Edna. I'm sure God put the thought into your mind. Shall I ask Brother Wilmer if the church would be willing to fast and pray with us tomorrow?"

Edna nodded wordlessly, with tears in her eyes. She listened as John spoke to Brother Wilmer.

"Brother Wilmer said the same burden was also on his heart," John said as he replaced the receiver. "He said they will put the message on the prayer hot line. I think I'll stay home from work tomorrow if Abner can let me off."

The next morning Edna knelt quietly beside the bed

while her heart raised a wordless plea. Throughout the day, she and John took turns caring for the children. "Lord," Edna prayed repeatedly, "speak to my father. Break the hold the devil is using to keep him from finding You." What a comfort it was to know that the same request was being made in many homes.

At six o'clock that evening, John and Edna were kneeling in prayer together. Edna felt a rest, a sense of quiet peace and exuberance fill her spirit as she prayed. Was it the promise of God that her prayer was being answered?

John raised his head to look at her. "Edna," he said softly, "I think we should go over to see Father now. Can you get ready? We'll drop the children off at my folks."

Edna hurried to bundle the children into their wraps, while John scraped the van windshield. After the children were left in Grace's care, John and Edna turned toward Sam Yoder's farm.

"What are you going to say, John?" asked Edna.

"I don't know, Edna. We'll just go, and God will tell us what to say."

John and Edna opened the side door quietly and walked into the kitchen. Through the doorway, Edna saw Father sitting in his recliner with his Bible on his lap. As he looked up, Edna was struck by the peaceful look on his face.

"Father," she exclaimed, "how are you?"

Sam smiled. "This has been a good day," he said. "All day I have been hearing the verse that you often tell me, 'The blood of Jesus Christ his Son cleanseth us from all sin.' About six o'clock, it suddenly dawned on my mind that the verse means just that. I do not have to figure anything out. Just as you have been telling me, Edna, I only need to claim the blood of Jesus for my salvation."

"Have you asked Jesus to save you, and have you given your life to God, Father?" asked John.

"Yes, I have," Sam answered, "and He has answered. The turmoil is gone now, and my heart is at rest. But I would like to talk to Brother Aaron. Can you call him?"

Edna's heart sang for joy as John left to contact Brother Aaron.

"Father," she said, her voice trembling, "at six o'clock I was praying, and a joyful peace came to me. Then John thought we should come over here. Did you know our whole church is fasting and praying for you today?"

Sam could only shake his head. When he spoke, his voice was awed. "No," he said, "but we cannot understand the workings of God."

Mary knelt beside her husband and wept.

"Would you like to go along, Edna?" John asked. "Some of the youth girls will keep all the children for the couples from church that want to go."

"I've never been to a big city to help in street evangelism before," said Edna, "so I would like to go. But do you think it would be good to leave the children again?"

"Well," said John, "not for just anything. But Father has been doing so well that you haven't needed to leave the children anywhere for two months now. We would be gone for about eight hours. That's about long enough, but I think it could work. It's your decision."

"Then I'll go," said Edna. She turned from the soup she

was stirring and looked up. "John, do you think Father's improvement had anything to do with the prayers of God's people when we fasted for his salvation?"

John nodded quietly. "It could easily be," he answered, "and you know how Father has been praying for time to reach all of your siblings for the Lord. God does answer prayer."

With a light step, Edna boarded the bus with John the next Saturday. Music rang through the bus as it traveled toward the city. As they approached the city, Brother Wilmer stood up to give directions to the group.

"We're going to start out in the park," he said. "So most of you will be singing. John, could you please stand beside the tract rack? A few of us will circulate in the crowd to answer any questions."

Edna looked at the people who walked by in front of the group. Some stopped to listen to the songs the group sang. Some, with blank and hardened faces, merely glanced over and hurried on. But a few stopped and listened with rapt attention. Edna watched as David Martin and Jared Weaver, two young brethren from the congregation, handed out CDs.

After an hour, the group moved to a sidewalk location near the city transit station. People poured out of the building, some going this way and some that. John and Edna stood at a street corner, offering tracts.

"God bless you!" an elderly man exclaimed.

"No!" a young woman snapped. "Keep your religion. I have my own." Edna was horrified at the sinister look of her black clothes, the cold look in her eyes, the green hair.

A lady, with two children walking and one in a stroller, approached. Edna reached for a child's packet. She looked at the children's CD inside the bag. How many godly songs would be floating from the windows of dilapidated apartments tonight? It was a pleasant thought.

At two o'clock, the group boarded the bus again and started home.

Brother Wilmer stood up at the front of the bus. "Does anyone have a personal testimony to share or a prayer request for someone you met today? We have two hours to make good use of. We'll start from the front on this side and work our way around the bus. Young men, we'll start with you."

"I met a man who said he was Tom," one of the young men shared. "He said he's a Jew, but he asked us to pray for him."

"We'll do that," said Brother Wilmer. "What other prayer requests do you have?"

"I'm so grateful for salvation," Sister Rose shared, when it was her turn. "When you stand on the sidewalks and watch the masses of ungodly people flow past, you can't be thankful enough for God's gift to us."

Edna nodded, and a smile unconsciously graced her lips.

"Well," said John as they drove home in the van, "I'm glad we went. Are you, Edna?"

"Yes. I'm glad to share the Gospel and glad to work with a group of consistent, godly people. It's such a blessing to see serious Christians simply doing what churches should do, with lives that are quietly in order—like an engine that runs without coughing and sputtering."

"Exactly!" said John. "Did you notice that all the young men had their suitcoats on? And acted decent and consistent?" John paused a moment to think. "Our clothes are a part of showing the world who we stand with. So wearing plain suits to do street evangelism is certainly appropriate," he continued. "These boys aren't ashamed to identify with the separated people of God."

"I know what you mean," answered Edna. "And as we learn to know the young men, we find that most of them are committed to a consecrated Christian life. John, let's make sure we raise boys who know God, who know how to pray and live selflessly for God."

"Amen!" echoed John.

CHAPTER 24

"I'm really looking forward to today, John!" Edna said, putting the bacon on the breakfast table. "I'll be glad to get my quilt out of the frame. But the thing I'm really looking forward to about the quilting today is the fellowship with so many of our friends. I haven't seen some of our Meadow Brook friends for a while."

"How many are coming?" asked John as he salted his eggs.

"Helen, Christina, Betty, and Judith are coming for sure," said Edna. "Ruth really wanted to come, but her children are sick with the flu. None of the other ladies are coming."

"So then you have room for about four more people around your quilt frame," John commented. "How many did you invite from our congregation?"

"You're right." Edna smiled. "I did invite four more—Esther Mast, Susan Miller, Rachel Troyer, and Denise.

They're all coming."

"Well, I hope you have a good day," John said when he left the table. "I'm going out on the truck today, so I might be home a little late."

Edna sang softly as she washed the breakfast dishes. Sarah began to cry.

"How is my little girl this morning?" Edna kissed the warm cheek as she lifted Sarah from her crib. "Did you know you'll have lots of little friends to play with today?"

Sarah banged her spoon on the highchair tray as she waited for Edna to bring her breakfast. Then she ate industriously—as she did everything else.

"Children," Edna called up the stairs, "it's time for everyone to get up. Get dressed and come down for breakfast. Then we'll need to take Rachel, Paul, and Hannah to school."

Before long, the children all trooped into the kitchen. "I'm getting big," Mary said, cutting her pancake. "I can go to school next year."

"You're doing your preschool book," said Rachel. "So you're already getting big, Mary!"

Mary nodded happily.

"Shall I read you a book when I come home tonight, Mary?" asked Hannah. "Sister Susan said I may have my turn to bring it home tonight. I can read all the words in it! It's about Sam. He was a lad who sat in the sun."

"That's exciting, isn't it, Hannah?" said Edna, looking into the first grader's eyes. "Will you read to me?"

Hannah nodded vigorously as she chewed a mouthful.

"I want egg!" exclaimed Conrad as he pulled on Rachel's sleeve.

"All right, little brother," Rachel said. "But don't get my school dress dirty! Are you going to play with Justin today?"

"I imagine you will, Conrad," said Edna. "Did you know we're having company today? Ben and Justin are both coming, and we'll share the toys with everyone."

Conrad clapped his hands as well as he could with a spoon in his right one. Quickly Edna grabbed his flailing spoon. "Eat your breakfast now," she said.

Edna breathed a sigh of relief as she walked back into the warm kitchen after the trip to school.

"I want you to watch the little ones now, Mary. What would I do without my helper?" she asked as she patted Mary's head. The little girl's face glowed with satisfaction.

Conversation flowed freely around the quilting frame. The house rang with the noise of little children.

Susan Miller lifted two-month-old Sylvia from her carrier and began to rock her. "Your quilt will soon be finished, Edna," she said. "I don't see how you get so much done."

Edna laughed. "Really, I didn't do most of this quilting. But I am looking forward to having space in the living room again. I think I'll invite some more of the sisters next week. Maybe we can finish it that day."

Crying and scuffling erupted from near the toy box. Rachel Troyer turned her head toward the dining room. She rose quickly and hurried to the scene.

"Justin," she said firmly, "no! You cannot hit Ben." She withdrew to the bedroom with her son.

"Tell Ben you're sorry," Rachel said when they returned.

"I'm sorry," Justin said.

"That's all right," answered Ben. "Do you want to play with me now? We can play farm."

"We really miss you, Edna," said Helen, in a quiet moment together.

"I miss you too," said Edna. "I'm really glad to see you again. How is everything going?"

"Fairly good," Helen answered. "Did you hear that Moses and Sally had another baby last week?"

"No, I didn't!" Edna said. "I'm glad you told me. Anything else?"

"A few of us sisters are getting together to pray for our young people each week," Helen said, "and I really appreciate the encouragement of sharing together like that."

"Who comes?" asked Edna.

"All the sisters are welcome," said Helen. "But it's usually just Sarah, Ruth, Betty, and I. You're welcome to join us too. It's on Monday afternoon at two o'clock—at our place."

Betty sat down on the empty chair beside Edna. "I was so glad you invited me to help you quilt today, Edna," she said. "How has your father been?"

"The last months have been better for him," Edna replied. "Did you hear that he received the Lord?"

"We did!" Betty replied. "We were so glad!"

Edna looked around the quilting frame with a grateful heart. What a treasure it was to have caring friends who encouraged her in the Lord!

With Conrad holding his hand, John followed the usher up the church aisle. He and Conrad sat on chairs, and Paul on the end of the front bench. The Pine Ridge auditorium was certainly filling.

After devotions, the moderator stood up.

"We will give our attention to Brother Paul Miller now," he said.

Brother Paul stood up and surveyed the congregation. "Tonight," he said, "we are going to look at a subject that affects everyone here. We are all under authority, and most of us have some level of being in authority. Our subject is 'Law and Grace.' "

John listened attentively as Brother Paul warmed to his subject.

"Law becomes necessary because of our carnal natures," he continued. "Law has a vital place in bringing us to repentance and therefore to knowing God. Law teaches us that there are consequences to sin. Therefore, our human hearts are directed to God. When we have repented, God is able to meet us with grace. But law prepares our stubborn hearts to bow to Him.

"Neither could we do without grace. Without God's grace, there would be no tolerance for any of us before we come to God. Without grace, there would be no mercy after we have repented. For God doesn't owe us reconciliation with Himself.

"Law becomes necessary wherever authority is in place. God has commissioned government authorities to punish sin. Law becomes necessary in church life to bring the carnal one to an awareness of his sin. For without law, the carnal heart will not repent. It is necessary in our schools and in our homes if our children are to learn the fear of

God. Without law and consequences for sin, the human heart will not learn respect for authority. And where there is no respect for authority, there will be no fear of God.

"So we would say law is the precursor of grace. Think of a child. If the child is taught that it is more unpleasant to disobey than to obey, he will learn self-control and respect for his authorities. When he gets older, that respect for his authorities will make it easy for him to honor God. Then he will be controlled, not as much by outer restraint, or law, but by a new heart. Law was necessary before his heart was changed, but now his inner restraints are developing and grace is free to come into play.

"In church life, we see the same elements. A sincere Christian will have a heart that is already turned toward God and can be directed and blessed by grace—or teaching and encouragement. As truth shines upon a heart that is prepared, that heart responds with joy instead of resistance. And there is rest and blessing as man begins to act in harmony with God. The struggle is over. So law, which brought that individual to grace, is a means to abounding grace.

"A carnal heart acts in resistance to God. So when carnality shows its face in church life, and the individual will not respond to grace—or teaching and encouragement—it becomes necessary to bring that individual to an awareness of his sin through church discipline.

"Psalm 23 tells us, 'Thy rod and thy staff they comfort me.' The rod can be likened to law, and the staff to grace. Both work together to bring us into—and keep us in—communion with God."

After church, the brethren talked in clusters. John shook

hands heartily with Harold Steiner.

"I've been listening carefully tonight," Harold said. "How much should we need law in church life, John?"

"Well," said John, "we could also ask the question this way. Has God given authority to the church? Wherever there is authority, discipline must also be in place as consequences for violating law."

"I read an article by someone who proposed that he was a part of the 'new conservatism' that held the same values as the 'old conservatism,' " said Kent Mast. "But the writer's working agenda was different. Instead of approaching carnality with the 'harshness of discipline,' as he called it, he said godly values need to be taught by teaching and encouragement."

"But unfortunately," said David Miller, "I have observed that churches operating under that premise rarely keep principles more than one generation—if that long. And while they are faithful, they depend on disciplined thought that was put into place previously."

"I don't know of any churches that have a consistent practice without using discipline," said John. "Do you brethren?"

There was a general shaking of heads.

"John," said Edna as they sat on the sofa that night, "what are you thinking?"

"I'm thinking thoughts that are sort of an offshoot of the message tonight. Brother Paul told us that law brings us to repentance. He also said it is by God's grace that He works with us to bring us to repentance through law and to bless and direct us after we have repented.

"I've been thinking of an article I read last week. It said that if we are carnal and feed on sin, the grip of the sin element in our lives will continually grow stronger. If we crucify the flesh and deny our carnal desires, the sin element starves and loses strength. The writer put it this way. He said that appetites are embellished by familiarity."

Edna nodded. "Helen talked to me tonight. She hardly knows how to be at rest with the situation at Meadow Brook. Harold is still hoping things will come around. You know how wearing it is when there is a constant struggle because the standard is down at church."

"I do," John answered.

"Helen mentioned that shock is the first thing we feel when we see wrongdoing. But you can't really be alarmed all the time. So when things don't change, gradual acceptance sets in."

"I guess that's right."

"She needs to find rest in her spirit," said Edna. "But she's afraid she'll finally start accepting a relaxed position in relation to the problem issues that Brother Edward allows. And she doesn't want to become comfortable with sin. It tears her up emotionally.

"John," said Edna, "thank you for bringing us to Pine Ridge. I don't think I could handle a long period of time like our last years at Meadow Brook were."

"We're glad that God led us to Pine Ridge," said John, "and I'm grateful for a godly wife who is always ready to do the right thing."

Edna looked up and smiled.

CHAPTER 25

Edna stepped closer to the bed and leaned forward. She listened to Father's shallow breathing. It had been such a joy to watch Father grow spiritually during the last year. "Is he still breathing?" whispered Elizabeth, stepping closer with her sleeping baby.

"Yes," said Edna. "I'm so glad you could get here in time. Maybe he'll open his eyes again this morning."

Elizabeth nodded mutely as she wiped tears from her eyes. She handed the baby to her husband, Melvin Glick. "Mother said we should wake her if anything changes. Now what can I do to help?" she asked Edna.

"We're just watching him now," said Edna. "But if you'd like to, you could put a little Vaseline on Father's lips."

Eagerly Elizabeth reached for the container.

John came over to Edna. "Shall we sing for Father?" he asked.

"He always liked that," said Edna. "I'm sure he would

now. He's resting quietly, but he probably hears us."

Softly the assembled family sang Sam's favorite song. "He leadeth me: O blessed thought! / O words with heavenly comfort fraught! / What e'er I do, where're I be, / Still 'tis God's hand that leadeth me."

Sam's eyes opened, and Edna leaned toward him. "We're here, Father," she said, pressing his hand. "We all love you!"

Sam smiled faintly. His lips moved.

"Yes?" asked Edna, leaning closer to hear.

"Thank you . . . for leading me to . . ." Sam paused. Then, with an effort, he began again. "To God. The blood of . . . of Jesus . . ." Then his voice faded away, and his eyes closed.

Edna stood up and cast a quick glance at Elizabeth, who hurried to the bedroom to waken her mother. In a few moments, Mary came to the bedside.

"Sam," she said softly, taking his hand. "It's Mary. I love you!"

Again, Sam opened his eyes. They focused on Mary's face, and the trace of a tender smile touched his lips. Mary sat by the bedside, holding Sam's hand. Two hours later, Sam's breathing became ragged and more irregular. "Edna!" whispered Mary. "Look at his face."

Edna's breath caught in her throat as she looked at the beloved face. For a full minute, it lost its worn, haggard look, and a beautiful smile relaxed Sam's features. Then the haggard look returned—Sam was gone.

Edna wept softly as John moved to her side.

"He smiled, John," she said. "Did you see the light on his face?"

"I did." John's voice choked. "Maybe he was . . . seeing Jesus."

Edna watched as Steven and the undertaker lifted her father's body from the bed and placed it on the litter. Then the litter was loaded into the vehicle.

Edna stood beside her mother, willing strength to her. The journey was over. Sam had gone home.

"Lord," prayed Edna, "thank You for saving my father. Thank You for the blood of Jesus."

"Shall I take you home, Edna?" John asked gently. "You didn't sleep at all last night."

Edna smiled gratefully at her husband. "All right," she said. "Elizabeth will be here with Mother the rest of the day."

The next three days passed in a blur. After months of helping to care for her father, Edna was numb. Vast numbers of friends and relatives came to the family home to share their sympathy. "I brought some potato salad," Mrs. Morris said as she pressed Edna's hand. "I'm so sorry about your father's passing. I'm sure he was a godly man. I admire you people."

"Father was a godly man because he came to know Jesus," Edna said softly. "The last words he spoke were these: 'the blood of Jesus.' And he died with a smile on his face."

"What a lovely way to die!" exclaimed Mrs. Morris. "Sometimes I think I might take God seriously."

"When we meet God, it will be the only thing that matters," Edna returned. "Thank you so much for coming. It means a lot. We'll enjoy the potato salad."

Then it was Stephen and Thelma. "We're so sorry," Thelma said as she shook Edna's hand. "I hear you have been so faithful to your father."

Edna's eyes blurred with tears. "It was my privilege to help. I'm so glad he came to know the Lord."

"Yes," Thelma said. "Stephen told me about that. We were so glad too!"

On the day of the funeral, John and Edna sat with the family in the living room near Father's coffin. It felt slightly strange to be in a Shady Glen service again. Edna watched Bishop Sam's face as he preached. How he was aging!

Softly the singing wrapped Edna's soul in comfort. The music of her childhood spoke of closeness and belonging. Today, with sympathy for the family's loss, the church community was more open to John and Edna.

As the coffin was lowered into the ground in the cemetery, John picked up Conrad. "Grandpa doesn't live in his body anymore," he explained. "Grandpa is in heaven with God."

The little boy watched uncomprehendingly. Edna held Sarah close in her arms and cried against her cap.

There was the grating of metal against earth as strong arms lifted the soil to cover the coffin—shovelful after shovelful. Edna watched tenderly as John and Paul each added several shovelfuls. Death was so final. This was the end. Father was gone! And the ache in her heart deepened.

Then a smile softened Edna's face. Father was gone for now, but it would only be a short time until they met him in heaven.

"Edna." It was Denise. "I'm so sorry. I know how it feels."

Edna nodded, and her tears flowed freely as she clasped Denise's hand.

"John," said Mary, "Steven thinks he would like to stay on and rent the farm. Would you help us work out an agreement?"

"Sure," said John. "That will work out nicely for both of you. Then he and Anna can be here for you. Or would you like to move over to our daudyhouse apartment? We have enough room for our family without that."

"I thank you," said Mary. "I know you would welcome me. But this is where I have always lived, and I think I'll stay here. I'll come over to see Edna when I get lonely."

"Does the daudyhouse need any repairs?"

"A few," said Mary. "Shall we go take a look?"

Edna glanced around the two-bedroom apartment. "It must be ten years since Grandpa lived here," she said. "I remember coming over to spend evenings with him."

"Do you want new kitchen linoleum, Mother?" John asked.

Mary nodded. "I guess it's about time for that, and a fresh coat of white paint on the walls will brighten everything."

John studied the kitchen. "Grandpa didn't need to do much cooking," he said. "But you will do more. Would you like us to put cabinets in front of the window? Then you would have an L-shaped kitchen and quite a bit more kitchen space."

"Father and I thought that was what we would do when we moved over here," said Mary. "Just match what's here as well as you can. I won't be particular." She paused and wiped a tear. "Things like that just don't seem important anymore. Cabinets are just . . . things," she finished.

"I know what you mean," said Edna. "Facing death with a loved one makes you realize what really matters."

John took his tape measure to the window. "I could move the sink over here so you can wash dishes at a window," he said. "We'd probably replace all the countertops anyway."

"I would like that," Mary agreed. "Then I can look out at the gazebo Father built for me just before he really got sick. We both enjoyed the flower beds around it so much."

"We'll all get together and houseclean the house for you," promised Edna. "Let's see. We have about two months until Steven gets married, don't we?"

"Yes," answered Mary. "We can do the housecleaning and painting in here in the next month. Then I can move out of the main house to give Steven time to do whatever he wants to do there. If the cabinets aren't finished when I move in, it will be fine."

"You're sure you want to be alone?" asked Edna.

"I think so," said Mary. "Maybe I'll board the schoolteacher. And you and Steven's will be close. That means a lot to me, so I won't really feel alone."

Then Mary walked to the window, looked out at the gazebo, and sighed heavily. Quietly Edna squeezed her hand.

"John," said Edna as they drove home, "could we do something special in Mother's kitchen—as a gift from us?"

"What did you have in mind?"

"I really like the cross-corner lazy Susan you made in my kitchen. Would adding that be too expensive?"

"No," said John, "that would be fine. And if Mother is ever in a wheelchair, she'll have a lot of shelf space she can access."

Edna smiled happily.

CHAPTER 26

John moved toward the door with his school board notebook. He smiled at the children, who were playing Memory and putting a puzzle together at the kitchen table.

"You all have a happy evening—and be good for Mama," he added as he smiled at Edna.

"We will!" the children chorused.

"Will you be back in time for a snack?" asked Rachel. "We're having the cookies I made today."

"Probably not," answered John. "But I would love to taste one. Can you save one of your cookies for me, Rachel?"

"Yes," said Rachel. "Mama can give it to you when you come back."

John enjoyed the quietness of the drive to the school building, where the school board would meet. When he arrived, only one vehicle was there. Entering the basement, he found Austin Weaver.

"Good evening, John," Austin said as he greeted John. "The Lord bless you."

"And you," returned John. "So we're the first ones here."

"We are," said Austin. "I was hoping this would happen." He cleared his throat. "Jared is thinking about beginning a friendship, and he is wondering what you know about Doreen Kauffman."

John laughed. "Really, quite a bit. I know her about as well as I would know my own sisters. She has been our hired girl for quite a while. Edna always feels comfortable having the children in her care when she needs help. I believe she must be about twenty-five."

"Twenty-four," corrected Austin. "Is she a dependable worker?"

"Very much so," said John. "Edna says she just walks in and knows what needs to be done. Edna likes the comfortable way they can work together."

"Is she a sincere Christian?" asked Austin.

"Doreen is very humble and committed to God," answered John. "She follows the same values we hold here at Pine Ridge."

"So then you would give Jared the green light?" asked Austin.

"Yes," said John, "but only because I know Jared is a worthy man. Doreen shouldn't have anyone with qualities less than that."

The conversation closed as Brother Wilmer opened the door. After everyone arrived, the meeting commenced. Brother Carl Martin opened the meeting with prayer. After devotions, he introduced the agenda for the evening. "We have three issues to deal with tonight," he began. "One is to decide whether we should raise Brother David's wages to help compensate for the medical expenses they have had with the birth of their last baby. The second one has to do with the friendship between Kevin and Glenda, even though the teachers have been trying to curb the problem. And the third issue is planning for a field trip in two months. Is there anything else?"

"Sister Tania mentioned that she would like to go to a wedding in four weeks," Austin said. "It is a close cousin's wedding, and she is asking for permission and a substitute."

Carl jotted the fourth point into his notebook.

"First, we'll look at the wage situation," he continued. "I'm concerned about it because I don't think our teachers should have to quit teaching for financial reasons. Brother David has been here for four years now. We all know you can't save a lot of money on a schoolteacher's salary, and his wages will not cover the extra costs they ran into with their second child. He is wondering what he should do."

"We could do one of two things without affecting his wages," said Brother Wilmer. "We could cover the expenses from the brotherhood assistance fund, even though we usually don't cover maternity costs. Or we can take a special love offering from the congregation to help. I don't think we want him to get another job."

There was some discussion. "I make a motion that we lift a love offering and add whatever we need from the assistance fund to meet the need," suggested John. "That way the congregation will feel that we are more personally sharing a love gift with our teacher. Our children will also learn respect and appreciation as they watch."

"I second it," said Austin.

"All in favor raise their hands," said Brother Carl.

"Unanimous," said Brother Carl. "Now for the second issue. You remember how we told the teachers to address the friendship issue between Kevin Troyer and Glenda Mast sternly and to tell us if they don't cooperate and drop the friendship."

"Let's see," said Brother Aaron. "Are they in eighth grade?"

"Yes," said Brother Carl. "The children have been cooperating on the surface. Now Brother David found out that they have been passing notes at recess for the past month. I've talked to the parents. Rodney and Levi are both concerned and supportive, whether we decide to expel the children for three days or to use some other form of punishment. They will also monitor their son and daughter and take care of it from the home front. You will remember we had a problem with this last year too, when we moved Kevin into the lower-grade room and Glenda into the middle-grade room for two weeks. So this is the second major offense with broken trust and deceitfulness in the same situation."

"They are new Christians now," said Brother Wilmer. "So this also becomes a church issue."

After some discussion, Brother James said, "I make a motion that we expel Kevin and Glenda, since this is the second time around. Then the ministry can deal with the church issue."

The motion passed. A half-hour later the meeting adjourned.

"Well," said Edna, laying her Bible aside when John walked in the door, "I didn't expect you this soon. Did you have a good meeting?"

John looked at the clock. "I guess it is only nine-thirty," he said. "Yes, we did. We had a number of things to take care of, but the issues were obvious. So it didn't take too long to reach conclusions."

Edna smiled.

"Yes?" John raised his eyebrows.

"I was just thinking how you come home from school board meeting with such a different air than you used to," she said. "When we were at Meadow Brook, you came home worn out and distressed. But now you come home without even having a lot to say."

John laughed softly. "I guess you're right. It is very different. I almost forget how board meetings used to be. It makes such a difference when everybody is on the same page, knows how things should be handled, and willingly cooperates. It's easier to deal with problem families here, and non-supportive families don't have swaying influence.

"One family left the church here a few years ago. The children were having a problem with disrespect at school, and the parents didn't like the dress code," said John. "But they had to make a choice—either to support the school or not to send their children here."

"It's not that we don't run into any problems here," said Edna. "But usually they're taken care of as situations come up. I wish everyone would know the blessing of being in harmony with God and the brotherhood. We make our lives so miserable when we make choices around our own pride and selfishness."

"Yes," John agreed. "Jesus said, 'My yoke is easy, and my burden is light.' And that is so true!" Abruptly he changed the subject. "How old is Doreen, Edna?"

Edna looked up, surprised. "She's twenty-four. But why is that so important, John?"

"It's just that Austin was asking me questions about her tonight," John said. "He said Jared is thinking of a friendship with Doreen, and he wanted to know what she was like. Austin told me Doreen is twenty-four, when I had figured she was about twenty-five. I wanted to see if he was right."

Edna smiled. "They must have done their homework correctly. Did you say she's a fine girl?"

"I did. I think Jared is twenty. Is that right?"

"I believe so," said Edna. "That means Doreen is a little older, but it probably won't matter. Jared is mature."

"I would have married you if you had been thirty," John told her, a twinkle in his eye.

Edna laughed and turned to prepare John's snack.

CHAPTER 27

"Take your time when you visit the grave," said John. "I'll stay in the house with the children until you come back. I have some inside Saturday jobs to do anyway. I'll tackle your stove first."

Arriving at the cemetery, Edna braced herself against the bitter cold. She stepped out of the vehicle and walked quietly to her father's grave. One year had passed since she had watched the coffin being lowered into the ground. What a blessing to know that Father was in heaven! Edna stood with bowed head as she contemplated the passage of generations and time. Each generation needed to pass the torch of truth to the next one. How precious to have had a godly father. How she loved him!

"Lord," she prayed, "thank You for Your salvation for both my father and me. Help me to teach my children, by word and example, so that they too will follow You."

With a heart at rest, Edna turned homeward. Upon

reaching James and Denise's lane, she decided to turn in. Denise answered the door with a dustcloth in her hand. "Welcome!" she said. "How did you know when to come? I was just wishing for a talk with you."

"I went to Father's grave this morning," Edna answered. "It's a year now since he died, and John said I don't need to hurry home. So I decided to drop in a little bit and see Kara again. I can't stay long."

Denise led Edna to the bassinet. "She's six weeks old today," Denise said quietly. "I can hardly believe that she is really ours! We all love her dearly."

Edna smiled tenderly at the sleeping baby girl. "I'm so glad God sent her to you," she whispered with feeling. "Babies are such treasures."

"How does it feel, now that one year has passed?" Denise asked quietly when they returned to the kitchen.

Edna wiped away a tear, but she smiled. "I am at the stage of grieving where I am grateful that I had a godly father," she answered. "I am remembering the happy, good times we shared. Father and I had so many good talks while I was nursing him before he died. I treasure those."

"And your mother?"

"She's lonely, as you might expect. But she's doing as well as can be expected. John brings her over to spend the day with us about once a week. She's busy making a quilt for each of the grandchildren. Mother always was the kind to reach out beyond herself, so that helps now."

"She's a very precious mother," said Denise. "Can you sit down a little? James and I have something very involving to think about. You know how our congregation is planning to help establish a new congregation in Michigan for three seeking families."

Edna sat down on a kitchen chair and nodded her head.

"The ministry and the committee responsible for the new outreach are asking us if we will be willing to go to provide leadership. Then another minister would be ordained for Pine Ridge," said Denise. "So James and I are praying about it."

"I see," said Edna. "We surely would miss you, but we'll support you wherever God calls you. Somehow John and I were wondering if this might happen."

"The feeling of the committee is that our children are young enough that we can make the adjustments more easily," said Denise. "We are looking at it seriously. We wanted you and John to know. We've been through so much together."

Edna nodded wordlessly. Then she spoke. "We certainly have. Your friendship means more to us than words can say. But we'll be praying. And if you decide to go, we'll do anything we can to help you."

Edna drove home with heavy thoughts. How they would miss James's if they moved! But beneath the thoughts of that disappointment, there was an undercurrent of something deeper. She and John felt such a weight whenever the upcoming ordination was mentioned. Could it be that John would be called? What did God have for their future?

"Father," prayed Edna, "You know about everything in this situation. Thank You for the blessing James's have been to us. Use them for Your glory now. And we ask You to supply the needs of the one who will be called to replace the minister who moves."

Edna's face relaxed as a quiet peace filled her heart. God would provide.

Eight months passed. Brother Brendon stood up to face the congregation. "We all know that Brother James and Sister Denise plan to move to the new outreach in Michigan, along with Brother Carl and his family, and that Brother Jared and Sister Doreen will join the group after their wedding in a few months.

"Our next step is to ordain a minister to replace Brother James here at Pine Ridge. That has already been cleared with the same congregational decision that released Brother James. So we will proceed with that ordination in three weeks. We will have the qualification message before I leave for home this week. Then we will take names and have the ordination when my wife and I return in two weeks."

John was quiet as the family returned home. Edna glanced in his direction several times but said nothing.

"Edna," said John as they entered the house, "I think I'll fast and pray today. Do you mind taking care of the children alone?"

"No," said Edna.

The day passed quietly. Edna read Bible stories to the children in the afternoon. After supper, a car drove in.

Edna peered out the window. Then she walked to the bedroom door and opened it. "John," she said softly, "James and Denise are here. What do you want to do?"

"I'll come out," John answered. "An evening spent together will be a blessing."

The children played happily in the dining room and on the floor of the living room, while the couples settled down to chat.

"Did you find a house yet?" asked John.

"We have two possibilities we're seriously interested in," answered James. "When Denise and I go out next week, we'll make a choice. We like the property with the metal shop that I could use with my electrical business. So we have a lot of things to think about. But we believe the Lord is leading us to go, and He is opening doors."

John nodded, but said nothing. James waited quietly.

At length John spoke. "James," he said, "I trust you more than a brother. I have a question. Did you know that you would be ordained before it happened?"

James glanced at Denise. Then he turned back to John.

"Did we know?" he asked. "Not really. But we did feel a special burden as we approached the ordination. As I look back, I believe that was God preparing us. Denise also felt burdened.

"People have different testimonies. Some brethren did not think they would be ordained, but they were. And then you occasionally hear of someone who feels he received a definite message from God in advance. The important thing is to be in the will of God so that if God calls a man to the ministry through a faithful church, he is ready and willing to obey God.

"Are you feeling heavy, John?" James asked.

John bowed his head and nodded.

James was quiet, and then he cleared his throat. "I wasn't going to say anything, John," he said, "but God has been directing me to pray for you and Edna. Just be open to God, and whatever comes—know that He will be with you. Shall we pray together?"

A beautiful sense of God's presence filled the room as four hearts sought God and His direction.

"Lord," John prayed, "we ask You to be with James and Denise as they move to Michigan. Bless the work there. We pray that You will meet all their needs and make them a blessing. We ask You to be with the congregation here as another minister is ordained. Make him a blessing, dear God, and help us as a congregation to hold him up to You." John's voice choked, and he could not finish his prayer.

Edna watched quietly from the front seat of the church as Austin and John stood before the congregation, facing two songbooks. Inside one was the slip that would permanently change the life of the one who drew it. A holy hush fell on the congregation as hearts were lifted to God.

For a long moment neither man moved. Then Austin stepped forward and took his book. When Austin returned, John stepped forward and clasped the remaining one.

Brother Brendon came forward. He reached for Austin's book. Edna shut her eyes, waiting to hear what Brother Brendon would say. When nothing was said, she opened them again. By this time, Brother Brendon was reaching for John's book. Tears filled her eyes, and she drew in her breath sharply. So this was what God had been preparing them for.

"Lord," Edna prayed, "behold the handmaid of the Lord; be it unto me according to Thy word."

Brother Brendon spoke with feeling. "The lot has been found in the book of Brother John. Brother John, will you and Sister Edna please step forward."

As in a dream, Edna moved forward. She listened solemnly as John committed his life to God as a minister. Then they knelt together, and the bishops gathered around and placed their hands on John's head.

Edna's heart bowed quietly before God as Brother Brendon gave the charge. After the dedication prayer, Brother Brendon turned to the congregation.

"Brethren," he said, "let us pray for Brother John and his companion."

As the service closed, Austin and his wife, Sheila, were the first to greet John and Edna. "The Lord bless you, John," Austin said. "I will be your prayer partner, holding you up to God every day." He paused and blew his nose. "The Lord bless you indeed."

John nodded and gripped Austin's hand.

John preached his first message two weeks later.

"Brothers and sisters," he began, "the burden God has laid on my heart is probably an extension from the thoughts all of us have been having as we approached our recent ordination. My topic is this: 'Finding the Will of God in Our Lives.'

"As I look over the past years and see the way God has protected and led us, my heart is filled with gratitude. God's ways are past finding out, and when we open our lives to Him, He fills us with blessings that overflow."

Edna listened with a prayer in her heart.

Four weeks later John and Edna pulled out of James and Denise's lane with a loaded U-haul truck. James drove the second truck, while Denise and the children followed in a minivan.

"Are you ready to go to Oak Leaf, Michigan, Edna?" John asked brightly.

"Yes," said Edna, "I'm happy to do what we can for James and Denise, and I'm eager to see their new home and community." Edna pulled a few games out for Conrad and Sarah.

"You're quiet," said John when she said no more.

Edna looked up at John. "So much has happened, John," she said quietly. "I'm almost overwhelmed at all that is taking place in our lives right now. I guess it was good we didn't know all this would happen eight years ago when we started going to Meadow Brook."

John laughed softly. Then he sobered. "I'm sure it is, Edna. God knew what He was doing when He gave us one day at a time." He looked into Edna's face, willing her strength. "And He will also give us grace one day at a time," he added.

Edna nodded and smiled back. "I am so glad of that!" she replied.

The miles flew past rapidly. Just before two o'clock, the caravan pulled into James's new home.

John, Edna, and the children climbed out of the truck and looked around. "This is a nice place, James," John said as James stepped down from his truck. "It looks comfortable—like a family could feel at home here."

"I think we already feel that way," said James. He looked at Denise. "Don't we?" he asked.

"Yes," said Denise, "and we will feel even more that way after we empty the household truck and put our things where they belong."

Carl and Erma Martin emerged from the house, followed by brothers and sisters that John did not know. After introductions, everyone began unloading the trucks in earnest.

"Well," said John, as he, Edna, and the children traveled homeward the next morning. "What do you think of the little congregation here?"

"I really enjoyed learning to know everyone," Edna said. "The three families that requested help seem so sincere and humble. The sisters blessed me."

John nodded. "I found the brethren to be the same way. We'll be learning to know the congregation better when we come out to help with the services."

"How often will that be?" asked Edna.

"Brother Brendon said we can expect to come out about every eight weeks for the first year. The next time we can bring the whole family in our minivan. Shall we sing, Edna?"

John began singing, and Edna joined him.

"I would not have my way, dear Lord, but Thine;
I would not walk alone, for I might fall:
Thou knowest what is best, so lead me on;
I'll listen, Lord. I'll hear Thy faintest call.

I would not have my way, dear Lord, but Thine;
O keep me for Thyself and Thine alone:
When shadows fall and darkest night has come,
I'll trust in Thee to guide me safely home."

CHAPTER 28

John had just called the family together for family worship when there was a sharp rap on the door.

"Hello," said John as he opened the door. "Can we help you?" His eyes swept over a young couple and two small children standing on the porch. Were they selling something?

"John," the young man asked, "don't you know me?"

John studied the young man's face, so young—yet so worn by the hard knocks of life. And something about the young woman's starved face looked vaguely familiar.

"Remember?" the young man asked. "I called you Preacher John. And now I understand you are a preacher."

Sudden recognition burst into John's mind.

"Trent!" he exclaimed. "Trent and Rosalie! Come in. What brings you here?"

Edna stepped up. "Welcome!" she exclaimed. "What a surprise! Will you have seats?" she invited, motioning toward the living room. "Rachel, please find toys for the children. Rosalie, you will have to tell us the names of your children."

Rachel took the children to the toy closet, and the adults found seats in the living room. "What can we do for you, Trent and Rosalie?" John asked, surveying them kindly.

"It's a long story," said Trent, the hard lines in his face softening. "I'm sure you remember when Rosalie and I got married. Well, it has been a hard life for Rosalie. She deserved better than the life of drinking and drug dealing I got into. Sometimes it got too hard and she left me for a while. Then I would promise to do better, and she agreed to get together again. The children came, and with that a lot of responsibility."

Trent paused and wiped beads of sweat from his forehead. "We never had enough money, and then I would go back to drug dealing again. So I was in and out of jail. I just got out of jail last week, and when I went home to Rosalie, she told me she had had enough—that she was already in the process of divorcing me.

"Rosalie isn't what she used to be either, but she is still a good, principled woman," said Trent. "I was close to the bottom when I got out of jail. Life was hard! But when she said that, I was absolutely crushed. For years, I had not been listening to anybody. But God finally put roadblocks in my path that I couldn't get around.

"I left the house and went back to a park bench for the night—I had often done that before. And I prayed for the first time in years.

"The next morning I went back to the house to see if

Rosalie would let me talk to her. She did, and I promised Rosalie that if she would give me another chance, I would get right with God—and we would start over right. And if that didn't work, I would never bother her again."

Trent stopped and smiled at his wife. "And she agreed, so we're here. You invited me to come and talk one time, John—outside the church. Remember that?" Trent asked.

"I do," said John.

"And I've often wanted to do that. When I longed for a father while I was in jail, I thought of you. So we're here. I decided if I was ever going to be a Christian, I would do it right. I would be part of a church that was the real thing. Can you help us find God and sort out the mess we've made?"

"I'll do the best I can to help you, Trent," John promised. "And how do you feel, Rosalie?" he asked, turning to her.

"It's like he said," Rosalie began shyly, "I'm willing to give our marriage another try. And I'm sick of our old life too." Rosalie stopped and wept quietly. Then she looked up with a spark of hope in her tired eyes. "I want to come back to God, whether Trent does or not. If I don't do anything else, I at least want to be a good mother to the children."

Edna's heart rejoiced. She listened to John as he helped first Trent and then Rosalie to a relationship with God again. As they prayed, confessing their sins, the angels rejoiced.

"You have come back to God now," said John. "That is the most important step. What else can we do to help you?"

"We need to find a real church," said Trent, "and I'll have to find a house and a job. We're basically starting all over. Everything we have is in the car, except the debts and legal charges that are still against me. And I'm going to have a lot of restitution to make. We're going to see if we can sleep at Rosalie's home tonight.

"Could you begin by teaching me how to be a good husband and father?" asked Trent.

"We will," said John as he nodded his head thoughtfully. "But perhaps there's something else we should do. We have an apartment here that you could use for a few weeks until you get things together. And in that time, we can be close enough to help you as you work things out day by day. It sounds like there could be a good bit to resolve. Would that be helpful?"

Rosalie's eyes lighted up. "That would be wonderful!" she said. Rosalie turned to Edna. "I want to go home to my parents—but not looking like this," she said, fanning her hands toward herself. "Do you have any dresses and a covering that might fit me, Edna?"

"We'll certainly try," said Edna, "and if I don't have any that fit you, we can do some sewing together for you."

"Could we try right now?" asked Rosalie. "I want to go home tonight."

Edna nodded and led Rosalie into her bedroom.

"How do I look, Trent?" Rosalie asked, stepping out of the bedroom twenty minutes later.

"Like a Christian woman," her husband said approvingly, "and your face looks like you're a different person."

Rosalie smiled.

John and Edna spent a lot of time with Trent and his family over the next weeks as they restructured their lives. Trent began working at Brother Aaron's place of business. Andrew and Nettie bought a small house in the area and offered it to Trent and Rosalie. It was a happy day for Rosalie when she settled into it—like a nesting bird.

"John," said Trent when he and Rosalie came for supper one evening, "you know we've been attending church with you at Pine Ridge most of the time. Rosalie and I have been to a few others too. Of course, we went back to Meadow Brook the morning we made our confessions there. But we feel happy and settled to stay at Pine Ridge. I don't want a church that lets people do what I used to do at Meadow Brook. Rosalie and I agree about that. This time we're both serious.

"We want a church that stands for something—and lives it. But would Pine Ridge want people like us?"

John nodded. "We want redeemed people who know the Lord and are following Him in obedience. Isn't that what you're doing?"

"Absolutely," said Trent.

"Then you would be a blessing to us," said John. "We're imperfect people, who have been saved by the grace of God. But we try to follow God seriously and do His will in our lives. We keep learning about God together. That's where the blessing is."

"I was just thinking," said Trent. "I didn't come to God until I really hit walls. We're just learning how to discipline our children. Maybe God has to discipline us too. And if our parents or churches don't do that, maybe God has to stop us other ways, right?"

John nodded. "It's called law, Trent. Law brings us into the kindness and grace of God, where the Lord loves to share Himself with us. And if it wouldn't be for God's mercy, there would be no way of salvation and no opportunities for us to repent."

Trent smiled. " 'For God so loved the world, that he gave his only begotten Son, that whosoever believeth in him should not perish, but have everlasting life,' " he quoted. "Aren't we grateful for that? Now I'm not afraid of my Father." Trent paused and smiled tenderly at two-year-old Kelsie in his arms. "And my children are not afraid of me," he finished, with a catch in his voice.

Rosalie looked up from the sink, where she was washing dishes with Edna, and smiled at her husband.

CHAPTER 29

Edna took Sarah's hand and walked into the church auditorium. Rachel, Hannah, and Mary followed. Quietly they took their places and waited for prayer meeting to begin.

It had been another busy day. After taking her mother to the doctor, mending the pair of pants John had been waiting for, and hosting company for supper, there had been little time to catch up on anything else. Edna sighed and relaxed against the church bench.

John also settled on another church bench with the two boys. Life was so demanding that he also felt hard-pressed to meet demands. The ring of the telephone could mean a three-hour interruption anytime, day or night. There were financial obligations to be met for the family, the congregation to be fed and nurtured, and parents to care for. His brow creased. His parents were at the point of needing more assistance. Would it be best to bring them to the daudyhouse apartment, so it would be easier to care for them?

John also sighed. "Lord," he prayed, "fill my cup. It is empty. . . ."

Brother Aaron walked to the podium. "For the devotional this evening, I felt led to look at Martha and Mary. So often I need to refocus on the Lord in the middle of life's turbulence. We will read Luke 10:38 to 42.

" 'Now it came to pass, as they went, that he entered into a certain village: and a certain woman named Martha received him into her house. And she had a sister called Mary, which also sat at Jesus' feet, and heard his word. But Martha was cumbered about much serving, and came to him, and said, Lord, dost thou not care that my sister hath left me to serve alone? bid her therefore that she help me. And Jesus answered and said unto her, Martha, Martha, thou art careful and troubled about many things: but one thing is needful: and Mary hath chosen that good part, which shall not be taken away from her.'

"Christ wants our devotion," said Brother Aaron. "He wants the gifts of our hands. But first He wants our heart's adoration. He wants us to take time to notice Him and to share in communion with Him.

"But often we are too busy. Like Martha, we are doing things we believe to be important—and in doing those things, we forget what matters most. We must take time to listen quietly to God, at His feet. We must shut out the noise of life so that we can hear His quiet voice speaking to us. John 10:27 tells us, 'My sheep hear my voice, and I know them, and they follow me.'

"When we get too preoccupied with the things we are doing and forget to wait on God, we run uselessly. Then the work is our own and not God's. But when our lives are an extension of the Spirit of God, there is power and it bears fruit."

John's heart was smitten. Yes, he was far too busy! And though he meant to wait on God, too often he was emotionally weary when he needed a full payload of energy. Yes, it probably would be better to bring Father and Mother over, so there would be less running back and forth. He would discuss it with Edna and his parents.

He jerked his attention back to Brother Aaron.

"I'll take prayer requests now," said the deacon. "Are there any testimonies or thoughts you would like to share as well? The time is yours."

Trent spoke. "I want to thank God that He is helping Rosalie and me to reestablish our lives around Him. As I continue to work through difficult areas of restitution, please pray for me that I will be humble and open to God."

John was next. "Brother Aaron's thoughts have spoken directly to my soul," he said. "I find myself busy and wearied like Martha, when I need the strength of God that is found in quiet communion. I confess that I have been neglecting my personal devotional time. And I ask that you will pray with me that God will give me wisdom to know what to drop and what to do—and a quiet heart that still waits on God when it is necessary to be busy."

"Amen!" sounded from one and another on the brethren's side.

Edna searched her heart. Perhaps she should have made soup for supper. And perhaps her mother would be glad to occasionally drop the quilts she was making to help with

Edna's work when there was a lot of visitation to be done.

The congregation knelt in prayer.

"Lord," prayed Brother Austin, "we bring Brother John's request to You. It is the prayer of all of our hearts. Give Brother John the spiritual, emotional, and physical strength he needs to bear a heavy load with family and church responsibilities. He confesses that he lacks devotional time with You. Help him to set that time aside. And when life is busy and things cannot wait, give him a quiet heart that listens to you in the middle of the storm.

"We thank You for the blessing he and Sister Edna are to our congregation. Give them what they need and help us to support them."

John knelt quietly, receiving the blessing of caring brothers and sisters as they helped him reach upward to God. His heart swelled with love and gratitude to God— and to his brethren.

Emily Troyer approached Edna after church. "The Lord bless you," she said, as they greeted. "Rodney and I know you and John have a lot to do. If you like, Tina could help you one or two days a week. We don't care if she helps you or John's parents. And there will be no charge."

Edna's eyes filled with tears. What an answer to prayer! "We would be most grateful!" she exclaimed. "How can I say thank you enough?"

"You don't need to," Emily said quietly. "I know how you feel."

"Edna," said John on the way home from church, "would it be easier for us to help Father and Mother at their place or at ours?"

"At ours, John," said Edna. "But what would Bishop Sam say about their living at our place?"

"I don't know," said John. "The Lord will have to work that out."

"Emily offered Tina one or two days a week, without charge, to help either us or your parents. Isn't brotherhood sharing beautiful?"

"It is! That will really help," John affirmed. "I also appreciated Austin's prayer for me. You know he promised to be my prayer partner on a daily basis when I was ordained. And I feel that support so much. Sometimes I share my needs with him. But other times he just seems to know what I'm going through without my telling him."

John turned on the signal light to enter John, Sr.'s lane. "Children," he asked, "what song shall we sing for Grandfather before I put him to bed?"

" 'God Will Take Care of You,' " said Mary. "He likes that one."

Edna smiled. What a fitting song to sing when God had so amply refreshed their souls.

"What did Bishop Sam say about your moving over to our place, Father?" asked John as he pushed his father's wheelchair onto the sunny porch.

"We talked about it at length last week," John, Sr., said. "I told him that Mother and I feel it is about the only arrangement that will work, unless we move to one of the other children in another community. But I said that we would like to stay where we have always been. So he said he would talk to the rest of the ministry.

"Today Bishop Sam stopped in again. He said in light of our situation, they have no problem with our moving into your daudyhouse since we're coming to a stable situation. I could tell he respects you and Edna and appreciates your faithfulness in caring for your parents."

"Praise the Lord!" said John. "Are there any restrictions? We can easily turn off the electricity in that side of the house since it has its own panel."

"Yes," said John, Sr. "They would appreciate that. And he warned me to remain separate from the world and to be faithful, which by the grace of God we mean to do. He said that with nursing in mind, they would not enforce the ban. So we're ready anytime you are," he finished.

John whistled as he and Brother Wilmer carried the hospital bed into the apartment a week later. Gradually the daudyhouse began to look like his parents' home.

"Thank you, John." His mother smiled as he stepped into the kitchen to repair a cabinet-door hinge. "Father and I are so happy about this move. It will make things work better for you. And we will feel a lot more secure with someone around most of the time. It means so much to have a strong son to lean on." Grace's eyes shone gently into John's.

John smiled back. "We're happy to have you and Father here, Mother," he said warmly. "It blesses us to share with you. I'm just returning the kindness you've given me all my life."

CHAPTER 30

"I always treasure the times I can take you along when I have meetings, Edna," John said. "I really need your support, and it adds to the blessing the congregation receives when the sisters can share with the evangelist's wife. But we can't do that very often with a growing family and with Father and Mother here.

"You know I have to leave for Moses and Sally's church next week. If the school board lets us take the children out that long, would you like all of us to go? And could you monitor their schoolwork? I won't be able to help, since an evangelist is expected to do visitation, plus preaching."

"I understand," said Edna. "I just gave you to God again last night." She paused and looked into John's eyes.

He smiled back tenderly, knowing what the battle had cost her.

"But what about Father and Mother?" asked Edna.

"I talked to Trent. He said they'll be glad to move over

here and take care of them while we're gone."

Edna raised her eyebrows and then laughed. "All right," she said, "let's do it. It will take a lot of work, but our family needs the time together. And I would love to spend a week with Sally."

"How soon will we be there?" Mary asked for the eleventh time.

"It shouldn't be more than about ten minutes," John said. "Moses said they live fifteen minutes away from the church we passed not long ago."

What a blessing it was to share with Moses and Sally and their children! The house buzzed with people and many helpers. While Sally and her girls did the housework each morning, Edna taught school. Somehow the afternoons disappeared, and then it was time for church again.

Edna walked into the tiny church building on Friday evening. "I don't believe this place could hold more than a hundred people, John," she said. "Have you noticed how close the congregation is, and how much they depend on each other?"

John nodded. "They have to because hardly anyone has relatives here. I believe Moses said they have nine families now." He paused. "Yes," he continued, "I love to see how they have bonded together. And they're following God faithfully. Pray for me, Edna. I have a burden to bring encouragement to this little congregation, and the devil is trying to thwart that."

"I will, John," Edna assured him.

Edna spent the evening praying silently while John

stood in the pulpit, preaching the Word.

"Brethren and sisters," he said, "this evening we are going to look at the greatest promise in the Scripture. Turn in your Bibles to John 16:33. Life will be difficult, and we will have pain and burdens to bear. But Jesus knew that, and He promised a victorious way through. We will read verse 33."

" 'These things I have spoken unto you, that in me ye might have peace. In the world ye shall have tribulation: but be of good cheer; I have overcome the world.' God is not defeated or dismayed. Instead He promises a way through our trouble that will bring blessing and cause us to grow into Him."

Edna sat quietly, drinking in the promises of God. As she reached for God through the responsibilities she and John carried, there would be strength for every day. And then there would be blessings to give to others.

She sighed as contentment again filled her heart.

"Edna!" exclaimed John as they pulled into the parking lot at Pine Ridge. "Am I seeing right?"

Edna blinked as she watched a family walk toward the church door.

"Stephen and Thelma!" she exclaimed. "Really, John?"

"Let's ask God to make us a blessing," John said. "I feel so responsible when people depend on us for advice and emotional support."

"Like you often tell me, we just need to share the Lord, and He will carry the burden of the people we touch," said Edna.

"You're right," said John. "Let's see if we can get into the building before they sit down."

"Thelma!" Edna said warmly, reaching out her hand. "God bless you! We're so glad you came."

Thelma looked eagerly into Edna's face and grasped her hand. As she read the encouragement and acceptance in Edna's eyes, she relaxed.

"We're only having soup for dinner today," Edna said. "But if the hostess for today doesn't mind, we surely would like to share it with you. We have so much to catch up on."

"I'd love that!" Thelma exclaimed. "We want to tell you what God has been doing in our lives."

Edna listened eagerly as John preached the same message that had blessed her during the Wyoming revival meetings.

"Remember," John said forcefully, "First John 4:4 tells us, 'Ye are of God, little children, and have overcome them: because greater is he that is in you, than he that is in the world.' What a promise full of reassurance and hope for our tired minds and bodies! There is never a situation that God does not know about before we reach it, or one for which He has no solution.

"It is in bowing humbly to God and His will that we are able to claim the promise. We read in James 4:6, 'But he giveth more grace. Wherefore he saith, God resisteth the proud, but giveth grace unto the humble.' "

Edna pondered the thought of humility. What would Thelma think of soup for Sunday dinner? For a moment, she cringed. Then she smiled slightly. There were so many spiritual and emotional needs that she and John needed time

THE TORCH OF TRUTH

and energy for. By cooking simply, her life had become more manageable, and it made life easier for the children. Yes, offering simple hospitality was the right thing to do.

John welcomed Stephen and Thelma warmly when they walked in the front door at home.

"We are so glad to have you," said John.

"And we to be here," said Stephen. "Remember how you told us we would always be welcome in your home, John, the last time we snapped beans together?"

"I do," said John, "and I remember that visit. We really appreciated that you stopped in to share with us."

The discussion at the dinner table centered on lighter, surface things. After the children bundled up and went outside to play tag, Stephen launched into his story.

"I'm sure you're wondering about our journey," he said. "Nothing really jolting has happened lately. But Thelma and I have been doing devotional studies on the life of Jesus in the past months. And we see that Jesus openly and honestly stepped out to honor truth and do His Father's will. He refused to honor the flesh but steadfastly did the will of God. And we are hungry for more of God.

"I have been a Christian ever since the night we knelt together in your barn, John," said Stephen. "But as we told you when we stopped in to see you, we have seen so many people leave traditional settings and lose their spiritual moorings. Would we do the same thing?

"We've watched you and James in the last years. We saw you living faithfully and honoring your parents. So we took courage and came to Pine Ridge today."

John nodded. "What are you looking for in another

church?" he asked.

Stephen paused a moment in thought. "We want a church that takes God and spirituality seriously, where Christ is free to work and live in our hearts," Stephen said. "And we want a church that is just as serious about walking in Biblical patterns. I don't know how to say it. But God isn't honored when we say one thing and live another. God calls us to purity."

"I'm glad to hear you say that," said John. "It is the only formula that will work, because it is God's own." John walked over to his desk and picked up his Bible. He opened it to John 15.

"Stephen, will you please read John 15:5?" he asked.

" 'I am the vine, ye are the branches,' " Stephen read. " 'He that abideth in me, and I in him, the same bringeth forth much fruit: for without me ye can do nothing.' "

"I love that verse," said John. "Sister Thelma, would you please read John 14:21."

Thelma took the Bible and read softly, " 'He that hath my commandments, and keepeth them, he it is that loveth me: and he that loveth me shall be loved of my Father, and I will love him, and will manifest myself to him.' "

John took the Bible again. "These verses teach a concept that I call content and form. If the content of the heart is right, the form—or the way we do things—will also be pure. Impure water does not come from a purified fountain. As the Spirit of God cleanses and directs us, we choose to die to self and live by God's Word."

"And if we fail to do that," injected Stephen, "we die spiritually. Because God cannot tolerate sin. I was reading in Revelation 3 this morning." Stephen stopped and flipped to the right page in the Bible. He read, " 'So then because thou art lukewarm, and neither cold nor hot, I will spue thee out of my mouth.' "

John nodded. "Think of the horror of being rejected by God!" He paused and began again. "But when we are cleansed and totally given to God, the real joy sets in. No freedom is greater than freedom from the chains that drag man to selfishness, sin, and finally into hell. But we have to repent and give God our filthy toys before He will bring us into the heavenly places with Him.

"God calls us to abundant life, fruitfulness, and joy! He says, 'Abide in me.' And when we abide quietly in Christ, His Person flows through us, directing and blessing our whole lives. He lives within us, enriching and sustaining our lives—and we are fruitful.

"I also like John 15:11," John continued. " 'These things have I spoken unto you, that my joy might remain in you, and that your joy might be full.' God wants to give us Himself and all His blessings. He wants our fellowship."

"I can't fathom that," said Thelma, "but I want all of God's blessings."

"Do you have any advice for us as we choose a church, John?" asked Stephen.

John smiled. "I will return some of the wisest advice I have ever received. When I asked you that question nine years ago, you cautioned us to choose a church that deals with sin. I will say the same thing.

"When we were in your place, my father also gave us this advice," said John. "He told us to go without bitterness or resentment and not to argue with people or to defend ourselves. 'Let your lives be your testimony,' he said. Father also cautioned us to keep Biblical applications and appreciate conservative values. He said those would help to keep us stable—and they do.

"When we begin to question conservative values that have been based on Biblical principles, we put ourselves in danger of rejecting truth. It's a very deceptive thing that faces people who are afraid of legalism."

"I see what you mean," said Stephen, nodding thoughtfully. "Thelma and I are both grateful for a framework that will help us do the will of God. The advice your father gave you sounds just like him." He paused, and began again. "How is he doing? Could we visit with your parents before we go home, John?"

CHAPTER 31

Edna patted the bread dough into loaves and set them on the kitchen counter to rise. John would be happy to find fresh bread, warm from the oven, when he came home. Then she assembled Mary's birthday cake.

Edna had just returned from checking on John's parents when the doorbell rang. Dusting off her skirt, Edna opened the door. There stood Emma.

"Come in, Emma!" Edna exclaimed. "You're just in time to help me do the roses on Mary's birthday cake. Yours always turn out so nice. That's what Mary wants this year."

Emma laughed and entered the kitchen. Laying her coat on a chair, she picked up a decorator's bag, added a tip, and filled the bag with icing.

"How old is Mary now?" she asked, expertly shaping the red roses.

"Nine tomorrow," said Edna. "Hasn't a lot happened

for both of us since she was born, Emma?"

"Oh, it has!" exclaimed Emma. "Some good . . . and some bad."

Edna nodded and waited for Emma to go on.

Emma sighed deeply. "Edna, would you have time to talk a little this morning?"

"Sure," Edna answered. "Would you like to go into a private room, or is this all right?"

"This will be fine," said Emma. "I just don't want to take up too much of your time."

"I have all morning," said Edna.

"It's this," said Emma. "Several years ago, I told you about the problem I was having sticking with good standards."

"I remember," said Edna, "and I pray for you every day."

Emma's face brightened. "Thank you," she said. "I really appreciate that. Things are going about the same, except that the issues we face keep getting deeper. Abner feels that living by standards means we are trying to perform our own salvation. 'Those are filthy rags, Emma,' he tells me. 'Have you really prayed openly about that? Does God want you to earn your own salvation?' Then eventually, I agree to do what he wants to do to keep peace.

"It has been one thing after another in issues like clothing, entertainment, and bywords the children can use. Abner has very few convictions anymore that are different from what a worldly person would have."

"I can't imagine how hard that would be, Emma," Edna said softly. "Does Abner give you a choice in the decisions?"

"He says we'll make them together," said Emma. "But

then he pressures me emotionally until I usually give in and agree to what he wants to do. You know how persuasive he is."

Edna nodded.

"We're not going to Living Waters anymore," continued Emma. "Now the issues my husband is trying to put into place are joining a Pentecostal church, getting a TV, and dropping the veiling. And I don't know what to do." Emma sat down at the table and wept softly.

Edna sat down beside her and waited quietly.

"Edna," burst out Emma, "does a woman need to sell her soul to obey her husband? Does she have to violate what the Bible says to please him? Does she need to help her children go wrong or to watch helplessly while they do? I have been pushed and pulled for so long that I hardly know what is right and wrong anymore."

Edna prayed quietly for wisdom to help Emma find her way. "It is God's will that we reverence our husbands," she said. "So honor Abner in any way that you can. However, when an issue is wrong or leads you or your children in that direction, you as a Christian woman are responsible to obey God instead."

"So I don't have to join a Pentecostal church to please my husband?" asked Emma.

"Do you believe joining the Pentecostal church is honoring God's Word?" asked Edna.

"Oh, no!" said Emma. "I know that it isn't."

"Do you believe that it would be right to have a TV in your home?" asked Edna.

"No, Edna," answered Emma. "It brings evil right into the home!"

"Do you believe 1 Corinthians 11?"

"Certainly, Edna," Emma answered.

"That's your answer, Emma," Edna said carefully. "We always need to honor God and His Word. The apostles said, 'We ought to obey God rather than men.' "

"I thought if I compromised on a few issues, Abner might become satisfied with where we were in our applications," said Emma. "But there doesn't seem to be an end. And it is so devastating to see most of our children going the wrong way."

"I can imagine," said Edna. "But you can be faithful. And when you are faithful, you have the opportunity to touch your children, to a great extent."

For a few minutes, the kitchen was quiet as Emma pondered the thought.

She finally spoke. "Edna, I know what I should do. I'm going to go back several steps to doing what I know is right. To drive a stake, I'm going to write those things in my journal. And I will do whatever I can to teach my children what is right.

"Edna, pray for me. It will be hard for me to be emotionally steady and not to get confused again. And it will be hard work to put a separated life in place again. But I'm going to wear a cape dress again, I'll stop going to the movies, and I'll only put on the right kind of music." Emma paused and then began again. "And I will need to find my way to a consistent church where I can place my membership. I have that right, don't I?" Emma raised her eyes to meet Edna's.

Edna nodded and smiled reassuringly. "You're one of

God's children, and the Bible teaches us to be a part of a consistent church. Then your brothers and sisters can support you and help you find your way.

"John puts it this way," Edna continued. "All earthly authority is authority under God's authority. When an authority steps out in unfaithfulness from the authority he is under, then we must go directly back to divine authority. We are always responsible to God. The bottom line is to do what is right."

Emma sighed deeply and settled back into her chair.

"I'll communicate with Abner about what I'm doing," she said. "I'll tell him and God that I'm sorry for the compromises I've made. By God's grace I must be faithful to His Word." Emma paused. "I don't have to agree to doing anything wrong," she finished slowly as a smile spread over her face.

"No, you don't," Edna said quietly. "I was thinking . . . What are some tender things you can do to show Abner that you love and honor him during your return to Biblical practices?"

Emma smiled. "I see what you mean. Any suggestions? I'll make sure I do five things each day—like having a warm cinnamon roll ready for him at breakfast, straightening his clothing drawers, writing a note of appreciation for something he did, and that sort of thing."

"You can follow his preferences where right and wrong is not an issue," said Edna, "and you can cultivate a meek and quiet spirit in any situation. And you can keep on praying fervently for him. That is a wife's most precious gift to her husband."

Emma nodded as Edna squeezed her hand.

"Do you mind if we get together and pray sometimes?" asked Emma. "That would mean so much to me."

"I would love that," said Edna. "We'll be prayer partners."

Long after Emma was gone, Edna stood at the kitchen window, gazing unseeingly in deep thought.

"John," she said that night, "doesn't Abner know what is right and wrong anymore?"

"I don't know, Edna. When we are deceived, we don't."

"It frightens me, John," said Edna, "to think that Abner started out fully intending to do God's will but kept going wrong because . . ." Edna stopped, and her sentence hung in the air.

"Because he failed to follow the Word, Edna," finished John. "We must always follow the Word. It is the torch of truth that God gives us. May God keep us faithful."

"Denise wonders if we're coming out this weekend," said Edna. "Is it our turn to go to Oak Leaf, John?"

"Yes," answered John. "They're having revival meetings, and Brother Brendon thought it would be good if one of us would go to give our support. Does it suit you to have lunch packed on Saturday? We can be there in time for supper."

"Sure," said Edna. "Denise said Doreen has been asking to have us to supper."

"That sounds good," said John.

Edna relaxed against the seat of the van as they traveled toward Michigan. She glanced back at the children and smiled contentedly.

"Happy?" asked John.

"Yes," answered Edna. "I was just thinking how nice it is to have this time alone with our family. Did you notice how they're all growing up so fast, John?"

"I have," said John. "We have a thirteen-year-old daughter now."

Rachel looked up from the book she was reading and smiled at her parents.

Edna sat down on the church pew beside Denise and waited for the service to begin. As she joined in the singing, her heart was drawn heavenward. " 'Mighty God, while angels bless Thee,' " the congregation sang in worship together.

After John had shared devotions, Brother Larry Kauffman stood up to face the congregation.

"Brethren and sisters," he said, "tonight we have come to meet with God, the Creator of the universe and the lover of every lost soul. God longs to know each of us, and He wants us to share in fellowship with Him.

"Tonight we are going to look at 'Fellowship With God.' God created our souls for fellowship with Himself. In the Garden of Eden, God came to walk and talk with Adam and Eve in the cool of the day. God also comes to share with us when we are consecrated to Him.

"To be consecrated is to be set apart. When our hearts are consecrated to God, we are set apart from the world. Then God is able to share Himself and what He is with us.

"There is also a fellowship that we share together as sons and daughters of God," said Brother Larry. "The Bible tells us that if we love God, we will also love one another."

Brother Larry reached into his pocket for his handkerchief and wiped his perspiring brow.

"Our hearts must follow after God," he continued. "The way we view God will determine how much He can bring revival into our hearts, our families, and our churches. It will also determine how much God can share Himself with us.

"To walk with God is to walk into the joy of eternity, where the strength of His vine flows into us and leads us into heavenly places that only a renewed heart and mind can understand. In the end, it is not costly to follow God. But it is the ultimate catastrophe not to."

John jotted notes into his notebook. Gratitude welled up in his heart. What an unfathomable opportunity to have fellowship with God Himself. And what a blessing to share with brothers and sisters who followed the Lord obediently and encouraged him in the Lord! He looked at Paul and Conrad on the bench beside him. For a moment his eyes swept over the pew where Edna and the girls were sitting.

"Lord," he prayed in his heart, "help me to lead my children to know You so that they will honor You with the fear of God in their hearts. Help them to walk freely into the loving arms of Your mercy when You call them, and bring them into fellowship with You. Lord," he prayed fervently, "help me to be faithful in holding forth Your torch of truth so that they will know and follow You. Lord, lead my children to follow You."

The tender melody of 'Just As I Am' filled the church house as Brother Larry opened the invitation. John's spirit was stirred in worship to God.

"Is there someone who has never known God who would like to make peace with Him tonight?" Brother Larry asked after the first verse of the song. "Or anyone who would like to renew fellowship with God that has been broken? Raise your hand or stand to your feet. We will sing another verse." Brother Larry nodded to the song leader.

" 'Just as I am, and waiting not / To rid my soul of one dark blot,' " the congregation sang softly.

There was a movement at the front of the sister's side, and Rachel stood to her feet, her head bowed.

John glanced at Edna, and for a moment their eyes met. Edna smiled and wiped a tear from her eye as she answered the joy in her husband's face. The torch of truth was being passed!